VIOLET AND THE
PIE OF LIFE

Violet and the PiE OF LIFE

DEBRA GREEN

HOLIDAY HOUSE · NEW YORK

π

HOLIDAY HOUSE is registered in the U.S. Patent and Trademark Office.

Printed and bound in January 2021 at Maple Press, York, PA, USA.

www.holidayhouse.com

First Edition

1 3 5 7 9 10 8 6 4 2

Library of Congress Cataloging-in-Publication Data

Names: Green, D. L. (Debra L.), author.

Title: Violet and the pie of life / by Debra Green.

Description: First edition. | New York : Holiday House, [2021] | Audience:
Ages 8–12. | Audience: Grades 4–6. | Summary: "When twelve-year-old
Violet's dad walks out, she faces the aftermath the only way she knows
how: with pie and math. But family and friendship turn out to have are
more variables than she thought"— Provided by publisher.

Identifiers: LCCN 2020009971 | ISBN 9780823447558 (hardcover)

Subjects: CYAC: Family life—Fiction. | Theater—Fiction. | Middle
schools—Fiction. | Schools—Fiction. | Mathematics—Fiction.

Classification: LCC PZ7.G81926 Vio 2021 | DDC [Fic]—dc23

LC record available at https://lccn.loc.gov/2020009971

ISBN: 978-0-8234-4755-8 (hardcover)

TO JEFF GARFINKLE, THE COURAGE, BRAINS,
AND HEART AT THE END OF MY RAINBOW

VIOLET AND THE PIE OF LIFE

ONE

$\mathcal{I}$ knew my parents could solve most of their problems by applying simple math.

The night when everything went wrong started problem-free. Great, actually, once Dad came home. I was in my room, but I heard Dad at the door because our house is only 875 square feet, and my dad is never quiet. "Who wants a bucket full of heaven?" he asked.

I hurried to the front of the house, inhaling the delicious smell of fried chicken along the way.

Dad stood grinning at the door, holding a large fast-food bag. He hugged me with his non-bag-holding arm and said, "Vi! The apple of my eye! You hungry?"

"Now I am!" I said, following him into the kitchen.

Dad pulled out a bucket of fried chicken and plopped it on the counter. "Your mom's not here?"

1

I shook my head. "She's at that listing appointment she was all excited about."

"Some people have a passion for music. Some for doing good. Your mother has a passion for real estate." Dad laughed. "Hey, let's each sneak one piece of chicken before she gets home."

I stared at him. It sounded like fun, but not if Mom found out. She was into family dinners—with the whole family, not two-thirds of it. I loved fried chicken, but it wasn't worth hearing another argument.

"Come on, Vi," Dad pressed. "It's killing me to resist this smell! If I can't sneak a piece of chicken, I'll keel over and die." He stuck his tongue out and clutched his chest.

I laughed. "The smell is driving me completely crazy," I said. "If I can't sneak a piece of chicken, my brain will explode."

"We can't let that happen. You know how your mother feels about messes. For her sake, you'd better eat." Dad opened the bucket, pulled out a thigh, and bit into it. "Ahh," he said.

I took a drumstick, ate a mouthful, and said "Ahh" too.

"But seriously, don't tell your mother," Dad said.

"Don't worry. I won't." If Mom saw us—eating without

her, leaning against the kitchen counter, talking with our mouths full, not using napkins—*she* might die.

"The only thing better than eating fried chicken is eating fried chicken with my favorite girl," Dad said, and I grinned at him.

I'd finished about 80 percent of my drumstick when I heard a car in the driveway. "It's Mom!" I whispered.

"Toss the chicken bones! Wipe your hands!" Dad said.

We rushed around the kitchen, two laughing fools.

"Admit to nothing!" Dad said in a loud whisper.

Mom walked in right as I was throwing paper towels over the evidence in the kitchen trash. She smiled. "What's so funny?"

"We're just deliriously happy to see you," Dad said.

Mom raised her eyebrows. That didn't ring true. Not lately anyway. Then she pointed to the bucket on the counter while she put her hand on her hip. "Why didn't you tell me you were picking up dinner? I defrosted turkey cutlets."

"You're welcome," Dad said unwelcomingly.

Mom put her other hand on her hip, doubling the unwelcomeness. "Did you go to the market for eggs and broccoli like I asked?"

"Does every word out of your mouth have to be a nag?" Dad said, frowning now.

"Does every word out of your mouth have to be a complaint?" Mom complained.

That's where math should have come into the picture. My parents should have stopped right there and determined how many words from Mom's mouth actually were nags and how many of Dad's words were complaints. Mom nagged a lot, but she also talked about real estate and the weather and other boring stuff. And Dad's complaints were totally outnumbered by his funny stories. One simple division calculation for each parent could have shown them that they did a lot more than nag or complain.

Or my mom could have solved most of their problems simply by reversing her nag-to-compliment ratio from this:

$$\frac{\text{NAGS}}{\text{Compliments}}$$

to this:

$$\frac{\text{Nags}}{\text{COMPLIMENTS}}$$

Unfortunately, my parents weren't interested in my mathematical solutions. Last time I'd suggested one, Dad had laughed as if I were joking and Mom had apologized for arguing in front of me. At least my math proposal had distracted them from their fight.

"I love fried chicken," I said now, trying the distraction technique again. Also, I was still hungry. I put my nose in the air and said in a snooty voice, "Such excellent cuisine."

My parents laughed.

My mom said, "Quite so!"

It wasn't that funny, but I faked a laugh to keep the household mood up.

"Let's eat," Dad said.

Mom put the bucket and sides on the kitchen table, I got the ketchup from the fridge, and we all sat down.

Then Mom tried to ruin things again. She said, "Do three people really need a large bucket of fried food?"

Before Dad could respond with his usual line that nothing he did was ever good enough for her, I said, "Yes, three people need a large bucket of fried food when one of those people is me."

To prove it, I grabbed another thigh and drumstick from

the bucket, drowned them in ketchup, and wolfed them down.

"Slow down, Violet," Mom said, frowning. "You'll make yourself sick."

Dad winked at me. "It's impossible to slow down with such excellent cuisine."

I winked back at him, poured out more ketchup, and grabbed more chicken, even though I already felt like I might throw up.

It was worth it though, because Dad put his arm around my shoulder and said, "That's why I bought a large bucket," and Mom said with a smile, "Twelve years old, ninety-something pounds, but she eats like a linebacker."

Dad laughed and went with it, speaking in a deep, dramatic voice like a sports announcer, "Violet Summers, newest, youngest member of the Chargers. Best known for her fierce tackle and her charming smile."

I grinned, and my parents grinned back, and I clutched my stomach under the table.

π

I felt even more throw-up-y later that night in my bedroom when the fighting started again. I could hear it through my door.

The thing about math is that it's logical. You have to solve the first part of a problem before going on to the next. Once that's figured out, you keep moving on until you have the whole problem solved.

My parents' fights were the opposite. They started arguing about one thing and moved to another and then another. Nothing ever got solved. In fact, it seemed like everything was getting worse.

I sat at my desk and added my parents' latest argument to my chart to see if I was right.

INTENSITY
OF FIGHTS

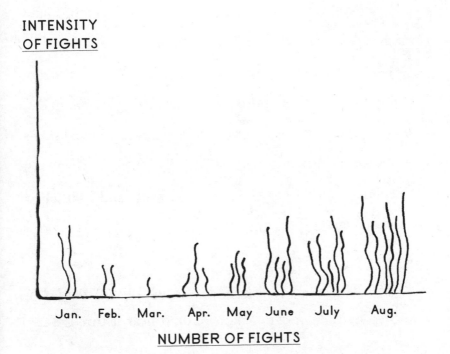

Jan. Feb. Mar. Apr. May June July Aug.

NUMBER OF FIGHTS

I stayed there, frowning down at the chart while my mom and dad shouted in the background. Finally, I put the chart facedown in a drawer, climbed into bed, turned out the light, and put a pillow over my head.

TWO

After school the next day, I sat in the back of the Horton Johnson Middle School auditorium with my best friend, McKenzie Williston. We were waiting to audition for the school play.

"It's so great that we're doing *The Wizard of Oz* this year," McKenzie said. "My dad played the Scarecrow when he was in high school. Did I tell you that?"

"Yeah." This was the third time she'd told me.

"I hope I get Dorothy," McKenzie said. "Go big or go home, right?"

I nodded, but I didn't want to do either of those things. I mostly wanted to hang out with McKenzie at rehearsals. And, hopefully, Diego Ortiz, who was sitting in the third row. I'd been stealing stares at the back of his gorgeous head. His hair was dark and thick and amazing.

Going big meant singing solo in front of hundreds of people. That was fine for McKenzie, but terrifying for me. I didn't like to stand out, not even for being good at something. For example, the odds that announcing my math skills would help my middle school popularity quotient were zero, so I kept those skills as secret as my crush on Diego.

I didn't want to go home either. Not if it meant hearing my parents fight again. Or hearing the front door slam late last night, and then a car driving off. Or trying to stay awake to hear the car return. Or checking for Dad's car this morning and coming up empty.

"I doubt I'll get cast at all," I said. I wasn't just being modest. There were so many kids in the auditorium, the ratio of auditioners to roles was at least two to one.

"You sing like a kitten," McKenzie said.

I wasn't sure what she meant by that. Soft and mewly? Or loud like a wildcat?

"On the plus side, you're pretty," McKenzie said. She must have meant the kitten thing as a minus.

I didn't feel that pretty. I liked my big brown eyes and peach-colored skin, the same combo as my dad. But my arms and legs were too skinny and long for my body. I was basically shaped like a spider.

McKenzie was softer and rounder. Nothing wrong with that. Pie was soft and round, and it was my favorite food. Plus, her skin was the same color as unbaked piecrust.

"Violet, you have to be in the play with me. It won't be any fun without you," McKenzie said. "What's a good non-singing part for you? Who's pretty in *The Wizard of Oz*?" I barely had time to think about it before McKenzie answered her own question. "The Good Witch. Does she sing?" Before I could answer *that* question, she said, "I don't think so."

Besides not wanting to stand out, the other reason I usually kept quiet was because McKenzie did so much of the talking.

McKenzie elbowed me. "Ugh. Look who's here.

I turned toward the door and saw Ally Ziegler. "Ugh," I said.

"She must have bought a new outfit just for this audition," McKenzie said.

Ally wore a blue dress kind of like the one Dorothy wore in the movie. McKenzie had on a blue dress too, but hers wasn't new. She'd worn it to fifth-grade graduation. It was pretty tight and short on her now.

McKenzie sighed. "Ally's going to be Dorothy."

"No way," I said, though there was definitely a way Ally would get cast as Dorothy. Easily. Ally wasn't just pretty—she was beautiful, with wavy black hair, creamy, copper-colored skin like in a tanning commercial, and huge blue, angelic eyes that looked like those sparkly quartz rocks in museum stores. Also, she was super popular, but not in a Mean Girl way. Everyone truly liked her.

Except McKenzie. And me, because I was loyal to my best friend. "Maybe Ally's a bad singer," I suggested.

McKenzie shook her head. "Ally Ziegler doesn't do anything bad."

She had a point.

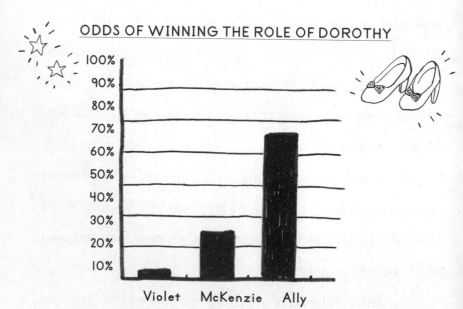

ODDS OF WINNING THE ROLE OF DOROTHY

Mr. Goldstein, the drama teacher, came in a few minutes later. He was short and balding, but he strutted up the aisle of the auditorium like a star quarterback taking the field. He passed the front row, turned to face us, and said, "Greetings, fledgling thespians."

"Couldn't he just say hello?" McKenzie whispered, and we both giggled.

Mr. Goldstein told us the girls had to sing two verses of "Somewhere over the Rainbow," and the boys had to sing the opening of the Tin Man's song. But he took a quadrillion hours to say it, because he also talked about each character starring in their own story and revealing our emotional cores and plumbing the depths of our inner beings.

At last, the first kid was called onstage. Poor Grayson Aljian sang just one line from "If I Only Had a Heart" before Mr. Goldstein told him to start over and project.

I definitely had a heart, and it was racing like crazy. Auditioning was bad enough. Getting interrupted and told to try again was terrible.

McKenzie nudged me. "Grayson will get cast because there's only, like, eight boys here. It's so unfair."

I nodded. There were around forty girls, so the boy/girl

ratio was one to five. Thinking about math calmed me a little.

But my heart raced again once Diego got onstage and started singing. He spread out his arms, which were long like mine, so they went really wide. He thumped his chest on every word of "If I Only Had a Heart," giving me the giggles again. Then he clutched his heart, sank to the floor in ultra-slow motion, and pretended to die.

Mr. Goldstein sniffed as if Diego were made of rotten eggs, and said, "I cannot say I agree with your humorous approach. The Tin Man is meant to be rife with heartache and longing."

Watching Diego made *me* rife with heartache and longing.

Ally came on next. Her voice was almost as beautiful as her face.

As Ally sang, Mr. Goldstein rose to his feet, which he hadn't done for anyone else.

He was silent afterward, even though he'd said "Thank you" or "Good job" to the other kids. A quadrillion years later, he finally said, "Your 'Somewhere over the Rainbow' gave me chills. Chills." He wrapped his arms around his chest, pretending to shiver.

"Get a hold of yourself, dude," I whispered.

"Told you she'd get the lead." McKenzie gave a long, dramatic sigh.

I wasn't sure whether I should agree with McKenzie or tell her she still had a chance. So instead, I joined in the sigh.

As Ally walked offstage, Mr. Goldstein said, "Let's see. . . . Who is next?"

Not me, I hoped. Not after the beautiful and chilling Ally.

"Violet Summers," Mr. Goldstein said. Of course.

"Knock 'em dead," McKenzie whispered.

I froze.

"Come on, Violet," McKenzie said, louder.

A few people turned around to stare at us.

"Violet Summers. Are you present?" Mr. Goldstein asked.

"You got this," McKenzie urged. Then she said, "She's coming, Mr. Goldstein!"

I left my seat and made my way to the stage in a slow daze, like Dorothy in the poppy field, and stood in front of Mr. Goldstein and, two rows behind him, Diego Ortiz.

"Stand tall," Mr. Goldstein said before I even started singing.

I straightened up, forced my mouth open, and began: *"Somewhere over the rainbow, way up—"*

"Positivity, Violet," Mr. Goldstein said. "Dorothy is a determined, joyful character. *Be* Dorothy. You're determined and joyful."

No, I wasn't. But I forced a smile so I could finish the song and get off the stage. I cleared my throat and sang, *"Somewhere over the rainbow, way—"*

"That is an improvement. Now show me your energy," Mr. Goldstein said.

Running out of the auditorium might show him my energy.

Instead, I stayed there and took a deep breath. On the exhale, I muttered, "Determination, joy, energy." Then I stretched my neck high as a giraffe and raised my nose in the air like a celebrity and plastered a smile on my face like Mom showing a real estate listing. The giraffe + celebrity + real estate agent combination must have looked really dumb.

"Superb," Mr. Goldstein said.

Okay, maybe not so dumb. And standing straight and smiling felt better than slumping and frowning.

I started singing and stopped thinking about how I looked or what the other kids thought of me, or even about Mr. Goldstein or Diego. I was Dorothy. I had determination, joy, and energy. The gangly girl who sang like a kitten had been replaced by a confident pro.

I sang two verses of "Somewhere over the Rainbow" while smiling the world's biggest smile and keeping my back perfectly straight. For those two verses, I liked having the attention on me. It felt amazing. *I* felt amazing.

When I finished, Mr. Goldstein nodded at me, and I could feel his positivity.

I bounded off the stage and down the aisle of the auditorium, grinning the whole way.

Once I returned to my seat, McKenzie patted my shoulder and said, "Great."

As soon as I was done freaking out about going onstage, I started worrying about my dad again. There were a lot of explanations for his disappearance, so that was good. But some of them involved criminal attacks and gruesome injuries and Dad lying in a ditch, so that wasn't good. The possibilities were getting complicated, so I opened my notebook, put my hand over it so no one (McKenzie) could see what I was doing, and tried to work it out.

"McKenzie Williston," Mr. Goldstein said.

"Knock 'em dead," I whispered.

McKenzie walked onstage with a huge smile, holding her head up and her back straight. She strutted like a runway model, except pudgier and about nine inches shorter.

I thought she sounded nice, but Mr. Goldstein didn't shiver or tell McKenzie she was superb or anything. Of course, he'd already heard two hours of auditions. As I told McKenzie, the world's greatest singer (Beyoncé, obviously.) could have performed at that point and Mr. Goldstein would have cut her off after two verses.

A few minutes later, after the last kid auditioned, Mr. Goldstein made a speech about how everyone performed wonderfully, blah blah blah, and not to take it personally if we didn't get cast.

"How are we *supposed* to take it?" McKenzie whispered.

"Yeah," I whispered back. Maybe I hadn't cared about getting cast before, but my audition had sucked me into caring. I'd imagined myself somewhere over the rainbow, starring in a play, and it had felt exciting.

Mr. Goldstein said he'd made up his mind about some

people today, so we might get a role even if we didn't get a callback. He'd post a list online tonight.

When we left the auditorium, I was grateful to see Grandpa Falls-Apart, our ancient Ford Mustang. Mom had a thing about being on time. That meant she was always telling me to hurry on weekday mornings, but it also meant never having to wait for a ride after school. Unless Grandpa Falls-Apart was acting up.

As I opened the heavy, dented car door, Mom said, "Does McKenzie need a ride?"

"Want a ride?" I shouted to McKenzie.

"No thanks," she said.

"It's getting dark!" Mom shouted.

"My mom's on her way. Bye." She waved.

I bet she wasn't coming.

McKenzie said her mother was in the Free-Range Kids Movement, which meant she believed in giving kids independence. When McKenzie and I first became friends in fourth grade, her mother would leave us at the mall for a few hours. We had a great time trying on fancy dresses and makeup, playing with stuff at the Apple store, and going the wrong way on the escalators. But my mom found out and ended our fun. She tried to make up for it by taking McKenzie and me to the mall, but it was completely different with her there.

Anyway, the Free-Range Kids Movement was great at the mall, but not so great if you wanted a ride home from school. McKenzie usually walked there and back. My mom didn't know that though.

Mom frowned. "I bet she's walking home."

Maybe she did know.

"I'll feel terrible if something happens to her," Mom said.

"Nothing's going to happen to her." I looked out my window. Mom was right. It *was* getting dark. I'd feel terrible too. "Get in the car!" I yelled to McKenzie.

"It's no problem driving you!" Mom said.

"My mom texted me she's coming," McKenzie insisted.

"By the time she's halfway home, the sun will be down," Mom muttered.

"McKenzie isn't going to change her mind," I said. Once McKenzie decided on something, there was no going back. She stuck with the things she loved—and hated. For the three years we'd been friends, she'd loved Justin Bieber and the color red, and despised Ally Ziegler.

Mom sighed and pulled away. Then she hit me with her usual quadrillion questions.

I informed her that school was good, lunch was good, and the audition was good.

"Well, good luck," Mom said. "Oh. I think you're not supposed to say good luck to an actor. It's like saying bad luck. I should say break a leg. Or maybe that's just before a show."

I didn't respond.

Then Mom did something weird. Weird for her, anyway. She stopped talking. No rambling about up-and-coming neighborhoods in Orange County, or open houses full of looky-loos, or condos that smelled like cat pee. No more about my day. Mom didn't even ask me about my homework.

Something was very wrong.

I looked at her hands. Yep. The hand that wasn't on the steering wheel was picking at her cuticle.

What if Dad hadn't come back last night?

I texted McKenzie.

Text to McKenzie: R U walking home?
McKenzie: Yeah

Violet: R U OK?

McKenzie: Fine. Jeez. U sound like ur mom

Violet: Sorry

I wanted to ask her to text me when she got home, but then I'd sound even more like my mom. I couldn't tell McKenzie I was worried about my dad. It would sound too whiny, since McKenzie was walking by herself in the almost-dark and her dad was dead.

"You know your father and I love you very much," Mom said in a choked voice.

Whoa. Where did that come from? I looked up from my phone.

"We've always wanted the best for you," Mom said.

"*Wanted*, as in past tense? You don't want the best for me anymore?"

"We do. We always will." She picked at her cuticle again. "Though it might not feel that way tonight."

We got to our house. A small U-Haul truck was parked in the driveway.

"What's that?" I asked.

"We'll explain." Mom sighed. "Well, your dad will explain.

He said he would. Although . . ." Her voice trailed off. Then she cleared her throat and said with fake confidence, "Your dad will try to explain."

THREE

SIGNS YOU'RE GOING TO HAVE A HORRIBLE NIGHT
Your mom gives you a dumb speech on the way home from school.

There's a U-Haul parked outside your house.

Inside the house is your dad, and his lips are quivering weirdly.

When you ask him what's going on, the weird quiver spreads to his entire face.

He says, "Sit down," in a froggy voice.

When you sit close to your dad on the couch, he slides away from you like you have a contagious rash.

His eyes start blinking fast and he says, "Vi, I'm moving out. I'm sorry."

He wouldn't look at me. Not because he was rude, but so he wouldn't cry. I could tell because of his quivery face and fast-blinking eyes and froggy voice.

"Why?" I asked, my face getting quivery and my eyes blinking fast and my voice froggy too. "Why are you moving out?"

Mom sat next to me and tried to put her arm around my shoulder, but I slid away.

He still wouldn't meet my eyes or give me a reason. I didn't count his croaky "Sometimes things aren't meant to be" line as a reason. If my dad asked me why I got a bad grade and I used that line, he wouldn't be satisfied either. Not that my dad asked me about my grades. My mom did that, and she did it more than enough for the two of them.

"Where are you going?" I pushed.

He didn't answer, not even after Mom said angrily, "Why don't you tell her, Will?"

"Can you look at me, Dad?" I asked. If he did, maybe he wouldn't be able to leave. "Please," I added.

He looked at me, finally. He didn't cry or even blink fast. He said, "Remember when you were worried about starting middle school, Vi? I told you moving forward is part of life. And you ended up liking middle school."

I shook my head. "I don't like it that much. And I miss my friends who went to other middle schools."

"You're making this so hard," he said.

"Me?" I asked, genuinely confused.

"It *is* hard," Mom said, still sounding angry.

"It's for the best, Vi," Dad said.

"Best for who?" My voice came out squeaky.

Instead of answering, Dad gave me a quick hug, stood, and walked out of the house like it was nothing.

It was the opposite of nothing. It was everything.

I wanted to run after him, grab his arm, and beg him to stay. But my dad wasn't the type to cave in to people. It would be like trying to give McKenzie a ride when she didn't want one.

He didn't even glance back.

I raced to my bedroom and slammed the door behind me, peering out my window as Dad drove off to the place where things were meant to be, wherever that was.

A minute later, I heard footsteps coming toward my bedroom and two knocks. I knew it was Mom, so I didn't open my door or tell her to come in. But I also didn't tell her to stay away.

She came in.

I kept standing and staring out the window. The darkness looked infinite.

Mom tried to hug me, but I squirmed away.

"I'm sorry," she said.

"You should be," I muttered.

I didn't want her to see me trying not to cry. I stood perfectly still, which was very hard work.

After about a minute, Mom apologized again, but this time she added my name, as if it weren't clear who she was talking to, and used her soothy voice, as if Dad had left for one of his short trips to Nevada, packing a duffel bag instead of a U-Haul.

Dad always went to Laughlin, not Las Vegas. He said you could stay in Laughlin for a third of the cost of Vegas and have just as much fun. Mom said he could *really* save money by not going at all.

One time we all went to Laughlin. Dad won big at blackjack and bought Mom opal earrings. Mom had said, "Great, now Violet will think gambling's a smart way to make money," but she was laughing and admiring her shiny earlobes in the motel mirror.

Now Mom said, sounding calm as a pond, "I want you to know we tried, Violet."

I couldn't help turning toward her. "Yeah, you tried! Tried

to get him to leave! Tried to nag him to death." Dad had said that last line a lot.

"Oh, Violet," Mom said, her voice full of pity. "I *am* sorry."

I'd never been apologized to so much in one night. As if a quadrillion sorries could make up for Dad leaving.

"I'm sorry too," I said. "Sorry you wrecked our family."

That got my mom to leave my room. She closed the door carefully behind her.

Then her footsteps were quick. Maybe she was rushing to her room to hurl herself on her bed in a sobbing heap of sadness. Maybe she was dancing around the house with joy. I didn't know. I didn't know anything.

I stayed in my room so I didn't have to face her. I'd already faced enough.

Luckily, I had everything I needed: my phone, my laptop, and food. Well, I didn't have TV. McKenzie had a TV in her room and could watch it whenever she wanted because of the Free-Range Kids Movement. But I didn't. And food meant an old bag of smooshed chips from my backpack. Still, eating stale chip crumbs beat having my mom treat me like a sad little victim.

My bedroom walls were pale blue, and my comforter was

violet. (Of course.) They were calming colors, according to real estate wisdom from my mom. Tonight, being surrounded by blue made me feel like I was drowning.

I opened my laptop to distract myself, but all I did was stare at the screen while thinking about the U-Haul and Mom's speech in the car and Dad telling me things weren't meant to be.

If my parents weren't meant to be together, then why did they get together in the first place and get married and have me? Even if they argued a lot, I couldn't imagine them not being together. They *were* meant to be.

And I wasn't just a sad victim. I could reunite them. I could pretend to be near death in the hospital and then wait for them at the entrance with romantic gifts like flowers, wine, and chocolate. I'd make a speech about how Mom and Dad loved each other and then watch them kiss and vow to be happy together. It would be perfect. Maybe.

PROBLEMS WITH PLAN TO REUNITE PARENTS

How could I get both parents to the hospital at the exact same time?

After finding out I'd tricked them into rushing to the hospital, my parents might be too mad to reunite.

I didn't even know if my parents liked flowers.

- Dad once said flowers were a waste of money.

You had to be twenty-one to buy wine.

- Mom liked wine, but Dad was a beer drinker.

- Beer didn't seem romantic.

Giving them chocolates could start another fight.

- Last Valentine's Day, after Mom joked about chocolate going straight to her hips, Dad had said, "I like your love handles," which somehow made Mom mad.

- If my parents fought even on Valentine's Day, how were they supposed to happily reunite?

I called McKenzie to tell her what had happened. Plus, maybe she could help me with my plan.

"Congratulations," she said flatly.

"Huh?" Congratulations for my dad moving out? Is there a greeting card for that?

"The callback. You didn't know?"

"We made callbacks?" I asked.

"Not *we*. *You*." She said it like an accusation. "Goldstein posted the list online."

"He did?" I asked stupidly.

"Ever since I got home, I've been refreshing the performing arts page on the school website every two minutes. You never gave callbacks a second thought. Then you got one and I didn't."

"I'm sorry," I said, like my parents had said earlier. We were a sorry family. "But Mr. Goldstein told us not to worry if we don't get a callback. He probably already decided that you're playing one of the leads. He probably called me back to see if I can even play a Munchkin."

"No. You gave a great audition. I can't believe you didn't even go on the website," McKenzie said, still sounding mad, but not *as* mad.

"My dad moved out. With a U-Haul and everything."

McKenzie gasped. "Oh, Violet! That's awful!"

Having your dad die was different than him moving away, but McKenzie understood the awfulness of not having a father around. "Why did he leave?" she asked.

"'Cause my mom kept nagging him."

"Ugh. I'm sure Ally got Dorothy, but maybe Goldstein wants me for something else. The Scarecrow should be someone tall and skinny, so that's out, and the Tin Man should probably be a boy since it's Tin *Man,* not Tin *Woman.* But I'd be good as the Lion."

She went on some more about the play, but I wasn't listening. I was busy thinking: *Isn't it rude to change the subject to auditions right after hearing about my dad leaving? Also: Don't you think getting a part in a school play is less important than your best friend's parents breaking up?*

But I didn't want to argue with McKenzie like my parents argued with each other. Look how that had turned out. Plus, I was a wimp. So I said, "I gotta go."

"That's sad about your dad," McKenzie said, almost as if she'd read my angry mind.

"Yeah," I said.

"Where'd he go?"

"I have no idea. He wouldn't tell me."

"Sheesh. Well, you should go to sleep. You have a big day tomorrow with your callback. If Ally gets Dorothy, I'll scream. And it won't be a scream of joy."

"Yeah. See you tomorrow. Bye." I threw my phone on my bed and sat there for a long time, staring into space—my broken-home space.

FOUR

WHAT WAS MISSING THE NEXT MORNING

Dad's shaving cream

His great-smelling cologne that Mom said was a rich person's cologne and we weren't rich

Beer from the fridge

The beat-up leather armchair

Dad's laptop, usually on the coffee table

All Dad's shoes from the hallway

Dad

Just standing in the hallway and seeing the floor, without his shoes, made me want to cry.

I must have been staring down too long, because Mom

said, "Are you okay?" with the same pitying voice from last night.

I held back tears and made my face hard. Then I pointed at the floor. "Happy now? You don't have to tell Dad to pick up his shoes anymore."

"No, Violet, I'm not happy. It's going to be hard for both of us."

I glared at her. What did she mean by "both of us"? Me and her? Dad and her? What about all three of us? What had happened to that?

On the way to school, Mom talked about her new real estate listing and the fall leaves and other fascinating stuff, while I stared out the car window at the gloomy fog. The plan I made yesterday, pretending to be in the hospital, was Swiss cheese-y with holes.

"Did you hear me, Violet?" Mom asked.

"Huh?" I turned my head toward her.

"I asked when the school play is."

"A couple of months from now."

The play! It wasn't like a giant light bulb suddenly lit up my brain . . . more like a sequence of little bulbs that made my brain brighter and brighter. When one bulb turned on, it lit up the next one, and so on, until I saw the light:

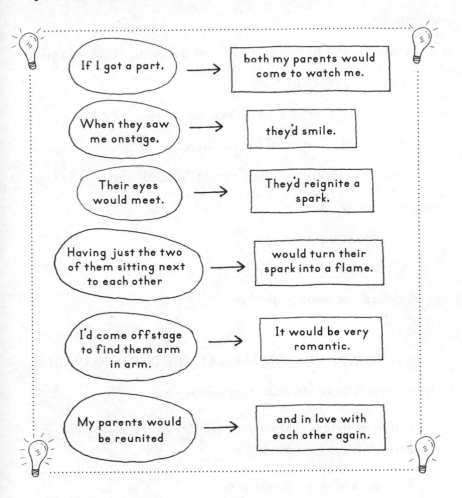

"Look, Violet." Mom pointed as we drove past a house even tinier than ours. "That was my first sale ever. Now the paint is peeling, and the yard needs sprucing up."

If she talked about her real estate listings to Dad in the auditorium, she'd never reignite a spark. She'd probably put him to sleep.

Once we got to my school, I asked Mom, "Can you pick me up today at five-thirty?"

"Five-thirty? Why are you staying—"

"Callbacks." I opened the car door.

"You got a callback! That's great, Violet!" she said as I got out of the car.

"So, can you pick me up?"

"Of course. Congratu—"

I closed the door behind me.

π

AUDITION ADVICE FROM MCKENZIE DURING LUNCH

1. Stand tall like Mr. Goldstein told you before.

2. If he criticizes your singing, tell him you're usually a lot better but you have a cold.

3. Beware of Ally's sweet act.

I stood by the back door of the near-empty auditorium for a minute, looking around, wondering why I'd been put on the callback list. The other kids had given fantastic auditions.

Ally, for instance. And Henry Tomaselli, who looks like what would happen if Harry Styles and Liam Hemsworth had a baby. And Sarah Blanchette, who always got solos in choir. But Diego Ortiz had gotten a callback too, after playing the Tin Man like he was doing a comedy routine.

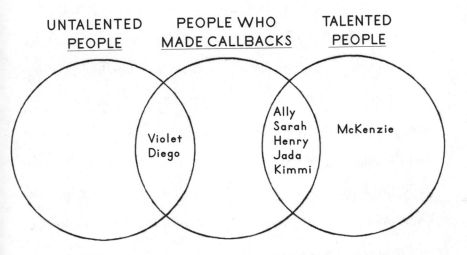

UNTALENTED PEOPLE

PEOPLE WHO MADE CALLBACKS

TALENTED PEOPLE

Violet
Diego

Ally
Sarah
Henry
Jada
Kimmi

McKenzie

I wondered where to sit. Sarah Blanchette stood behind the last row of chairs, doing weird voice exercises—*ahh ahh ahh ahh ahh,* like she was at the dentist's, and then *ee ee eee eeee,* like she was a martian. I couldn't wait to imitate her for McKenzie. Mamie Glassman paced up and down the left aisle, muttering, "You got this. You got this. You got this."

I slowly headed down the middle aisle. It felt kind of scary to do stuff without McKenzie. I wasn't used to it.

We'd been best friends since she joined my Girl Scout troop at the start of fourth grade. First, we'd had a circle of friends. *My* circle, really, made up of the girls who'd been in my Brownie troop and then moved onto Junior Girl Scouts together.

But McKenzie and I both quit at the end of fourth grade. As McKenzie pointed out when she was convincing me to quit, there's no reason to earn badges. It's not like earning money. It's only a piece of cloth for your mom to sew on your sash. (Well, for McKenzie's mom to *glue* on her sash. And after half the glue stopped sticking, for my mom to sew the badges on for McKenzie.) Also, McKenzie said the sash made us look like dorks pretending to be beauty queens. She thought the whole uniform was silly.

Anyway, quitting Girl Scouts made me spiral out of my circle of friends, which was fine because I had McKenzie spiraling right next to me. Later, the kids I'd gone through elementary school with split into different middle schools. I watched them spiral and scramble to make new friends while I clung safe and tight to my friendship with McKenzie.

Having only one real friend wasn't fine now, walking

through the auditorium, barely knowing any of the people I passed.

"Hey, Violet," Ally said. She was sitting on my right.

I froze.

She smiled and patted the seat next to hers.

Then the door opened, and Diego walked in. He stood at the entrance and said in a loud, high voice, "Here I am! Your Dorothy!"

Everyone laughed. My laugh surprised me. I hadn't laughed, or maybe even smiled, since I saw the U-Haul yesterday.

Diego rushed down the aisle behind me, calling out, "I have a feeling we're not in Kansas anymore!"

Before he could mow me down, I took a seat next to Ally.

She looked toward the back of the auditorium and whispered, "I didn't know McKenzie got a callback."

I turned around.

McKenzie stood at the entrance with her arms crossed, staring at me. Her gaze flitted to Ally and then right back to me.

I bit my lip and gave McKenzie a big, dumb shrug, as if I had no idea how I'd ended up here, as if I'd been unconscious and next thing I knew, here I was, at this callback McKenzie had wanted, sitting in a three-thousand-square-foot auditorium right beside McKenzie's mortal enemy, who was supposed to be my mortal enemy too.

McKenzie shook her head.

I didn't know what to do. I wished I could build a machine to travel back in time to choose a different seat in the auditorium. Or I could go farther back and skip the audition, or go way back and tell McKenzie to trust me, even if she saw me years later sitting next to her worst enemy.

To work out what to do, I did flowcharts in my head.

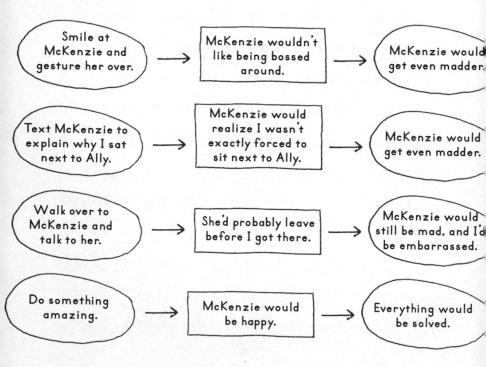

Smile at McKenzie and gesture her over. → McKenzie wouldn't like being bossed around. → McKenzie would get even madder.

Text McKenzie to explain why I sat next to Ally. → McKenzie would realize I wasn't exactly forced to sit next to Ally. → McKenzie would get even madder.

Walk over to McKenzie and talk to her. → She'd probably leave before I got there. → McKenzie would still be mad, and I'd be embarrassed.

Do something amazing. → McKenzie would be happy. → Everything would be solved.

Unfortunately, I couldn't think of anything amazing that would make McKenzie happy and solve everything. So I turned away from her. When I heard the auditorium door close, I sighed with relief.

"You nervous?" Ally whispered.

I nodded.

"Me too," Ally said, as if we had soooo much in common.

But we didn't have anything in common. It made sense that Ally got a callback. She was a beautiful, popular girl who probably had beautiful, popular parents and a beautiful house that was probably so popular Ally's family bought it in a bidding war.

So of course, with Ally's perfect life, she was guaranteed to make callbacks. But it was a total surprise that I did. And I had other things to be nervous about: McKenzie seeing me with Ally. My dad leaving. The real possibility that I'd start crying at any moment. Ally was probably nervous that she'd get the Good Witch or Scarecrow part instead of Dorothy.

When the back door opened again, I didn't turn around. What if McKenzie had returned? I was a wimp.

But it was Mr. Goldstein. He hurried to the front of the

auditorium and began talking. "Do you understand the theme of *The Wizard of Oz*?"

Duh. There's no place like home. I pictured my home this morning—its missing leather armchair, the bare hardwood floor. My home wasn't even like home anymore.

Sarah Blanchette raised her hand to answer Mr. Goldstein's question. I knew the right answer, but I wasn't a fan of being stared at.

"The theme of the movie is 'There's no place like home.'"

Mr. Goldstein said, "But remember, we're performing the play."

Sarah put her hand down.

I was so glad I hadn't raised my hand.

"An appreciation of the theme of *The Wizard of Oz* will help inform your auditions," Mr. Goldstein said.

Next to me, Ally started to yawn. She covered her mouth and tried to stop it, but made a little quacking noise.

I looked around to see if anyone else had heard Ms. Perfect quack. Diego was grinning and staring at Ally. I bet he'd heard.

I glanced back at Ally. Her cheeks were pink. She looked

like I would if I'd made that embarrassing noise, except prettier.

Mr. Goldstein kept going. "Dorothy is trapped on a farm in Kansas. The Scarecrow is tied up—literally. The Tin Man cannot move. And the Lion is paralyzed with fear. They each yearn to discover what they have deep inside them to propel themselves down the yellow brick road of life."

Ally yawned and quacked again—louder this time. A few kids stared at her. She turned bright red.

Too bad McKenzie wasn't around to hear that. She would have loved it.

Mr. Goldstein frowned and said, "Anyone unwilling to take this audition seriously should leave right now."

I actually felt sorry for Ally, for the first time ever. I changed my mind about telling McKenzie about her yawn-quacks, because now it just seemed cruel.

Mr. Goldstein connected speakers to his phone and played "Somewhere over the Rainbow." Then he had us listen to the Scarecrow's, the Tin Man's, and the Lion's songs.

Ally went onstage first and sang "Somewhere over the Rainbow" beautifully. I was glad McKenzie wasn't around to hear *that*.

When it was my turn, Mr. Goldstein handed me a sheet of paper with lyrics to the Lion's song in a big, bold font.

McKenzie had said she wanted to play the Lion if she couldn't be Dorothy. It would be a disaster if I got the part instead.

I opened my mouth, but nothing came out. I didn't have the nerve to sing "If I Only Had the Nerve."

"Do you want to be here, Violet?" Mr. Goldstein asked.

I nodded. I wanted to be here more than I wanted to be home with my fake-cheery mother and missing father and whirling brain.

"I mean *really* want to be here," Mr. Goldstein said. "Remember the theme. You're yearning, Violet. *Yearning.*"

I closed my eyes and thought hard about it. I did really want to be here, and not just to get out of my house and my head. I wanted to feel the joy and satisfaction I had yesterday onstage. And offstage, too, as I'd walked past the other kids. I, Violet Summers, had been noticed for something positive. I liked it. I wanted it to happen again.

But what I wanted more than anything was for my parents to sit together, watch me perform, smile at each other, and realize they should get back together.

"Mr. Goldberg, I really want to be here," I said.

"She *yearns* to be here," Diego said.

A few kids giggled.

I opened my mouth and sang the first words on the song sheet. I thought about my dad—his long, funny stories and his loud, easy laughter. I yearned for him. I sang and I yearned.

When I got toward the end, I pictured Dad walking through the front door, kicking off his shoes and throwing his arms around Mom, like I remembered him doing when I was little. Dad would call out "Vi, get in here!" and we'd have a family hug. As I sang, I stretched my own arms wide and then hugged myself.

Afterward, Mr. Goldstein smiled and said, "Splendid."

When I got back to my seat, Ally patted my arm and said, "Awesome!"

"Thank you," I murmured. I didn't want to come off as conceited, so I didn't add *I know I was awesome.* But I did know that.

FIVE

$\mathcal{I}$t was close to ten o'clock and I was already in my pajamas when the email came. I read it while sitting on my bed with my laptop, my door about 5 percent open because Mom doesn't let me use the internet in private.

Dear *Wizard of Oz* cast member:

Yes, cast member! This email signifies you won a part in our fabulous play. Congratulations!

We have a tight schedule. Starting this week, Ally, Diego, Sarah, and Violet will rehearse most days after school. Everyone else will rehearse once or twice a week. Closer to show time, the entire cast will rehearse four days a week and on Saturdays. Attached are the cast list and schedule. I look forward to working with you.

Sincerely,
Mr. Goldstein

After checking the cast list, I felt ... thrilled? Terrified? Shocked? Yes.

I got off my bed and paced. My room was ninety square feet, so I turned more than I walked. Even my familiar things didn't keep me from feeling so out of sorts.

Whatever *out of sorts* meant. I hardly ever felt calm. When my Girl Scout troop sang "Kumbaya" around the campfire, I hadn't felt peaceful. I was too worried about singing off-key, and the campfire embers starting a forest fire, and mountain lions. For me, being *in* sorts meant nervous and on edge.

I had to call McKenzie. That was the mature thing to do. Plus, it would be easier to talk over the phone tonight than face-to-face tomorrow at school.

It was my lucky night, kind of, because McKenzie didn't answer my call. So I left a voicemail.

"Hey, McKenzie. It's me, Violet. Obviously. So . . . Sorry for calling so late. Well, I . . . I'm sorry you didn't get the part you wanted. I hope you're not too upset. I didn't know I'd get cast as the Lion. I mean, I'm happy to be in the play, but . . . I'm sorry you didn't get a bigger part. Like Dorothy. Or the Lion. But, you know, playing a monkey will be . . . It sounds fun. I'm really, really glad you're in the play. Anyway . . . I guess . . . Did you hear that? Someone's knocking. So, okay. Bye."

For a second, I hoped it was my dad knocking. Sometimes when he came home late, he'd tap on my door to see if I was still up. If I wasn't already up, the tapping would *wake* me up. Then he'd lean against my desk or sit on the foot of my bed, and we'd talk.

Dad spoke to me like a friend. A friend like McKenzie, who talked more than listened, but he always had interesting things to tell me. Like the story of first spotting Mom at a restaurant where he used to work. She was meeting a blind date. Dad said he fell in love with her at first sight, so he pretended he was the blind date! He got Mom out of the restaurant before her real date could show up or his boss could blow his cover. It was super romantic, even though Mom tried to ruin the story during one of their fights. She said, "Even on our first date, you ditched your job and lied to me."

After a few minutes of Dad telling me stories like that, Mom would peek in the doorway and say it was past my bedtime and I had school the next day and blah blah blah. Then Dad would kiss my forehead, his breath smelling like beer and breath mints, and he'd leave. But sometimes he'd say, "Let me finish this one thing I was telling Violet about," and he would, and this *one thing* often would lead to one other thing and then another thing until Mom made Dad leave.

I'd also ask Dad for advice. He really understood me. And even if I didn't need advice, it kept him talking to me. After I told Dad about McKenzie wanting me to quit Girl Scouts, he said he'd only gone to one Boy Scouts meeting, because he'd found out the next event was a three-mile hike in the desert. Then I'd asked him, "So you think I should quit?" But before he could answer, Mom had stuck her head in the doorway and ruined things again.

Tonight, though, it wasn't my dad knocking. Of course not. If he came home late, he wouldn't come to *this* home anymore.

It was Mom. She opened my door halfway and leaned into my room. "Did you find out yet?" she asked.

I played dumb. "Find out what?"

"If you got a part."

"Yeah. I'm the Lion."

Mom smiled huge and put the rest of her body in my room. "That's wonderful, Violet! How exciting!"

I shrugged. "Well, it's not like I'm Dorothy."

"The Lion is a very big part!"

It was. I tried not to smile.

"How about McKenzie? Did she get a part?" Mom asked.

I nodded.

"What is she?"

"A monkey."

Mom raised her eyebrows. "A monkey?"

"Uh-huh. A monkey," I said. Then to change the subject—and because I really wanted to know—I asked, "Where's Dad?"

Mom stared at a spot to the side of me.

"Mom?" I said.

"I don't know."

"How can you not know where Dad is? You're still married to him, you know."

"I'm well aware of that," Mom said in a tone almost as snotty as mine.

"Is he within a ten-mile radius?" I asked.

"I don't know," Mom repeated.

"Maybe he left town so you wouldn't argue."

Mom sighed. "Maybe."

I didn't want to think about Dad leaving town or my parents arguing. So I said, "It's past my bedtime," which was probably the first time I'd ever uttered those words. It was probably the first time in history any kid had ever uttered those words.

"Good night. Congratulations." Mom backed away, closing the door behind her.

If Dad had come in, he would have told me a funny story. My favorite was about this waiter Dad used to work with who faked a French accent because he thought it increased his tips.

Then one of the customers started ordering from the guy in French. Dad laughed so hard at that, it took him three tries to tell me the end of the story: It turned out the customer was faking his French too. I started laughing with Dad. Then every time one of us stopped laughing, we'd look at each other and laugh some more.

Maybe one night soon I'd open my door, and Dad would be standing in front of me. He'd say that leaving us had been a giant mistake. The U-Haul would be in the driveway again, but this time Dad would bring his stuff back in.

If it wasn't past my bedtime, I'd call him.

Dad was probably awake, though, because he was a night owl. Mom was a lark. That's what she called getting up early and going to bed early. Dad once called it a stick-in-the-mud.

I decided to email him. We never emailed, but I was a better writer than talker. And I'd seen his email address on the school forms my parents filled out every fall and on permission slips for field trips.

I realized Dad might notice what time I emailed him and know I was up too late.

I paced my room some more while I figured out an excuse.

Then I sat on my bed with my laptop, opened my email account, clicked COMPOSE, and started typing.

Hi Dad,

Just woke up to get a drink of water and thought I'd send you an email.

I got a big part in the school play. I'm the lion in *The Wizard of Oz*. My best friend, McKenzie, got a part too.

I hope I can see you soon.

I stopped. If I emailed him tomorrow instead, I could delete the line about waking up to drink water, which seemed dumb.

But maybe Dad would read my email right away and get back to me tonight. If I waited until morning, he'd be sleeping. When he woke up, I'd be in school, so he might put off answering. Maybe he wouldn't answer at all. Which made me think I should ask him a question he'd have to answer.

But Mom had said he might be out of town. If he was in a different time zone, maybe he was sleeping now anyway.

If I waited until morning to email, I'd have trouble sleeping.

But if I emailed him now, I'd also have trouble sleeping because I'd keep checking to see if he'd responded.

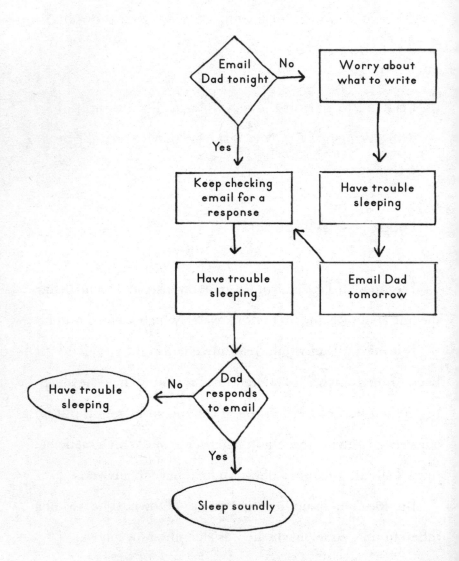

But if I waited, I'd have trouble sleeping two nights in a row: one night worrying about what to put in the email and the next wondering when Dad would write back.

I definitely had to send the email tonight.

I tried to think of another excuse besides wanting water, like a loud noise waking me. But I didn't want Dad to worry. Well, I sort of did want him to worry, but I didn't want him to think I was babyish.

I could write that I'd stayed up late studying for a test. But then he'd think I was cramming at the last minute.

Needing water seemed simplest.

I looked at my email again. Maybe I should add exclamation points after mentioning the play. But McKenzie said girls who used exclamation points were a "type," the same type who giggled around boys and wore ugly clothes just because they were in style—a bad type. Plus, if I added an exclamation point after writing about the play, I'd have to use one in the part about hoping to see Dad. Otherwise I'd seem more excited about the play than about him. I decided not to add any exclamation points.

I checked the time on my laptop. It was getting really late, much too late to wonder about punctuation.

I quickly typed the rest of the email.

You could email me. I mean, if you want.
Remember when we drove up to San Francisco and got clam chowder in bread bowls at the pier? We all stayed in the same motel room and you taught me poker and we played for M&Ms. You said when you won big playing real poker, we'd fly to San Francisco and stay in a hotel suite there and go to fancy restaurants.

Do you still want to do that? That would be really cool. Or we could stay at a motel again, because that was fun too.

Love,
Violet

I sent the email before I could think about it too much and chicken out.

Then I went to bed.

But I didn't fall asleep for hours and hours.

3 in a motel room > 2 in a hotel suite

SIX

MY MORNING IN FIVE SENSES AND FIVE EMOJIS

1. Seeing Mom's face close up: 😖

2. Hearing her say, "You slept through the alarm": ☹️

3. Smelling her morning breath: 😋

4. Feeling after finding no emails from Dad: 😣

5. Tasting the lump in my throat: 😝

I didn't have time to go to my locker before school, so I had to ask my first-period teacher if I could borrow a textbook.

"Violet Summers," Ms. Merriweather said as I approached her desk.

I was surprised she knew my name, since it was only September and she taught approximately 163 kids (five classes of about thirty to thirty-five kids each).

The bell rang. Once it stopped, I said, "May I please borrow the class textbook?"

Instead of handing me the math book, Ms. Merriweather said, "I was going to ask you to see me after class, but we might as well talk now." She spoke quietly, though I was sure the kids sitting near her desk could hear.

We might as well *not* talk now, not while my classmates were eavesdropping. That's what I wanted to tell Ms. Merriweather. Instead, I silently stared at my sneakers.

As I stared, I realized it was Mom's fault that Ms. Merriweather was embarrassing me in math class.

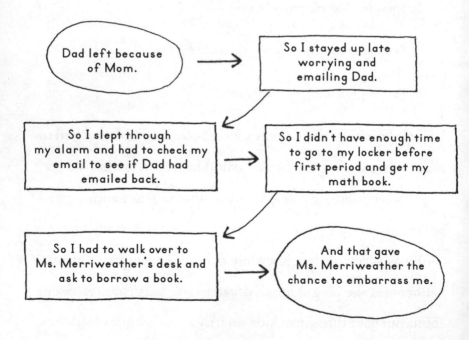

Dad left because of Mom.

So I stayed up late worrying and emailing Dad.

So I slept through my alarm and had to check my email to see if Dad had emailed back.

So I didn't have enough time to go to my locker before first period and get my math book.

So I had to walk over to Ms. Merriweather's desk and ask to borrow a book.

And that gave Ms. Merriweather the chance to embarrass me.

"I'm concerned about you, Violet," Ms. Merriweather said.

Uh-oh.

"Whenever I look over at you in class," Ms. Merriweather continued, "you're either checking your phone or doodling."

I'd hardly call creating mathematical charts of my life "doodling." But charts weren't in the syllabus, and the syllabus was what teachers cared about. So I said, "I'm sorry, Ms. Merriweather." Teachers cared about apologies too.

"Violet." Ms. Merriweather lowered her voice to almost a whisper. "Don't be embarrassed if you're struggling with the concepts."

I let out a snort, then tried to disguise it with a cough. The only concept I struggled with in math class was boredom.

My snort/cough made even more kids stare at me. Great.

"Instead of tuning out, raise your hand and ask questions," Ms. Merriweather said. "Or see me at lunch or after school."

I bit my lip to stop myself from snorting again.

"It's crucial to pay attention because the concepts build on one other. For instance, this week we'll be learning about pi. Next week we'll use pi to calculate circumferences of circles. Once we have that down, we'll calculate the volume of spheres."

I already knew all about pi. I'd found an amazing YouTube video about it a couple months ago and binged-watched and read everything I could about pi—which is probably the nerdiest thing any kid ever did on her summer break.

But there are so many interesting things about pi! It isn't just that pi and the best food ever—pie—sound exactly the same. Pi is infinite, with no patterns, no repetitions. Pi was first studied four thousand years ago and people are *still* trying to figure it out. Even computers can't figure out pi. In fact, calculating pi is used as a stress test for computers, because it can never truly be calculated. Dividing 22 by 7 is impossible.

"Violet, please pay attention." Ms. Merriweather handed me the loaner textbook. "And bring your book to class next time."

I walked to my desk, pretending I didn't notice everyone gawking at me.

Ms. Merriweather talked about pi while I forced myself to seem interested in her slow-motion explanation. My brain drifted as I stared at her. She didn't look like the other math teachers at our school, out-of-shape old white guys with ugly glasses and greasy hair. Ms. Merriweather was tall and muscular, like she spent her spare time lifting weights or playing lacrosse. She was young for a teacher, and her glasses had pretty turquoise frames. Her short, non-greasy magenta hair matched her magenta lipstick and looked nice against her brown skin.

Ms. Merriweather finally said, "Open your textbooks," so I slowly leafed through the loaner copy, stopping to read the graffiti: "Sam was here" and "Abby loves Ben." I wondered why anyone wanted to announce being in math class or declare their love in a textbook.

"This is way too hard," Logan Menendez said. "Someone should round pi to just plain three, because that's close enough."

"Yeah," Zelda Buchman said, "Pi has too many decibels."

Even though Ms. Merriweather had just lectured me about my "doodling," I couldn't resist making one simple graph.

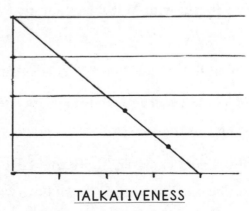

MATHEMATICAL INTELLIGENCE

TALKATIVENESS

When I finished, I looked up to find Ms. Merriweather towering over me, staring at my graph. I flipped over my paper fast. I wished I could melt into the floor like the Wicked Witch, to save myself from humiliation. I mouthed "Sorry" to Ms. Merriweather.

She raised her thick eyebrows at me. She had that trying-not-to-laugh expression McKenzie and I got sometimes in the back seat of Grandpa Falls-Apart when we texted funny stuff about my mom while she was driving.

When the bell rang, I rushed out of math class like it was on fire. I waited in the hallway for McKenzie, whose first-period class was two doors down from mine. Then we walked to my locker together.

It was my mom's fault that I hadn't had time to go to my locker before school started. So it was also her fault that I got to my locker with McKenzie, and that McKenzie saw the envelope.

She pointed to it and said, "What's that, Violet?"

"That" was small and white and taped to the middle of my locker.

Before I could answer, McKenzie walked up to my locker,

peered at the envelope, and announced, "It's not from a boy. Look at the writing."

I looked. My name was on the envelope in blue ink, with a large, straight *V*, a perfectly round circle dotting the *i*, another perfect circle for the *o*, a pretty loop for the *l*, and a smooth *e* and *t*. Two parallel, curvy lines swished underneath my name. McKenzie was right: not from a boy. Not that it would be. Even if a boy were interested in me, which was impossible, I didn't think boys sent notes to girls they liked.

I couldn't think of any girls who would send me a note either. No one besides McKenzie, but that careful writing— the perfectly round circles and pretty lines—definitely wasn't hers. Her writing always seemed like part of a ransom note or an SOS, scribbled in a state of emergency.

McKenzie tore the envelope off my locker, handed it to me, and said, "You can read it in private if you want."

"I don't need privacy," I said, because I couldn't imagine telling McKenzie I did.

But after I opened the envelope and we read the note, I wished I *had* asked for privacy.

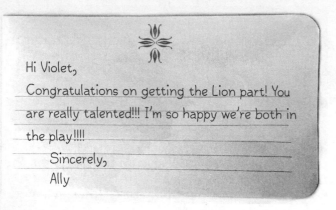

Hi Violet,

Congratulations on getting the Lion part! You are really talented!!! I'm so happy we're both in the play!!!!

Sincerely,
Ally

"Now I know why Ally's so popular," McKenzie said. "Phony compliments to make people think she's nice."

I felt my face tighten. Was it so hard for McKenzie to think of me as really talented? Or as a person who makes someone happy?

I glanced at her and noticed she was clenching her jaw. Maybe she felt that the beautiful, popular girl—the girl who had gotten the starring role McKenzie had wanted—was now trying to get her best friend, too.

So I said, "Sounds like Ally is desperate," and McKenzie relaxed her jaw a little. Then I said, "There must have been a sale at the exclamation point store."

I crumpled Ally's note and added: "Where's the trash can?"

McKenzie smirked.

Then I stuffed the note and envelope in my pocket and hoped there wasn't a trash can nearby.

SEVEN

$\mathcal{A}$s soon as school ended, I went to the nearest bathroom.

An eighth grader with raccoon eye makeup and black lipstick stood against the sink, painting her nails black.

I looked down to avoid eye contact. Clumps of wet toilet paper littered the floor. I dodged them as I rushed into the nearest stall, locked the door, and took the crumpled note out of my pocket.

As I reread it, I forgot about the scary girl at the sink and the bad bathroom smells and even my dad.

I didn't think Ally's four exclamation points made her seem desperate, like I'd told McKenzie. Actually, they made Ally seem kind of nice. (Anything more than four exclamation points might seem desperate though.)

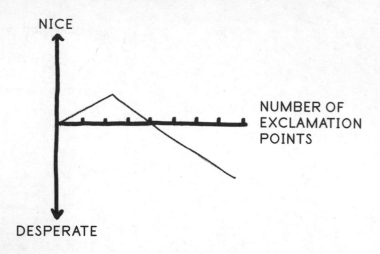

NICE

NUMBER OF
EXCLAMATION
POINTS

DESPERATE

McKenzie thought Ally acted nice to get popular. But maybe Ally simply *was* nice and people liked her for that.

When I walked out of the stall, I made eye contact with the girl at the sink, smiled, and said, "See you later."

"Hope not," she said, and spat at the floor.

I hurried out and checked my phone again. Nothing from Dad.

I got to the auditorium about two seconds before Mr. Goldstein, which was good timing, because he had us rehearsing right away.

We sang "We're Off to See the Wizard" a quadrillion times. Mr. Goldstein said we needed to sound peppier, except for Diego/the Tin Man, who needed to take it down about eight notches.

I thought he was in the perfect notch. He looked perfect too, wearing the long-sleeve red shirt that was my favorite.

"How about we compromise, and I take it down four notches," Diego said.

Mr. Goldstein raised his eyebrows.

"Five notches?" Diego asked.

Mr. Goldstein's eyebrows stayed raised.

I wondered if keeping your eyebrows raised so long would give you a headache, so I tried it.

"Now I'm annoying Violet, too," Diego said.

I dropped my eyebrows. I didn't have a headache, but my face burned with embarrassment.

"Okay, eight notches," Diego said.

"Let's move on," Mr. Goldstein said.

I couldn't move on. My brain was whirling.

SOME OF MY WHIRLING THOUGHTS

Does Diego really think he annoyed me?

Is it too late to tell him I wasn't annoyed?

Why had he been looking at me in the first place?

Where is my dad?

We each practiced our big solo songs onstage while every-one else watched from the front row. I'd thought it would be terrifying, but it wasn't. We clapped and cheered for one another as if living in Orange County, three thousand miles from New York City, was the only thing stopping us from starring on Broadway.

Mr. Goldstein dismissed Ally and me early so he could work with Sarah the Scarecrow and Diego. Ally and I stood together near the parking lot, waiting for our parents. We'd been so busy, I hadn't talked to her during rehearsal. Plus, I didn't know what to say. But now there was nothing to do but talk. So I said, "Thanks for the note."

"Oh." Ally paused, as if she felt awkward too. Which was ridiculous coming from someone so beautiful, so popular—someone who supposedly had dated a ninth grader. Then she said, "You're welcome. I was kind of worried I'd get the wrong locker, but I've seen you around there and I asked Lily Beggs, who was putting on lip gloss a few feet away, and she pointed to your locker. Mine is way on the other side of school. My locker, I mean."

If McKenzie were around, she would have said something like, "Does this girl ever shut up?"

70

But McKenzie *wasn't* around. She'd gone home after school. We—my mom and I—were going to pick her up for a sleepover on the way back from rehearsal.

"It's weird to send notes, huh?" Ally asked.

The weird thing was having Ally ask me whether something was weird. She would know the answer a lot better than I would. I probably did at least ten things a day that popular people like Ally automatically knew were weird and would never do.

"Your nose is crinkled up," Ally said, "like you're smelling a strong scent of weird."

I smiled. "My nose crinkles when I'm thinking hard about something. I guess I should think with my brain instead of my nose, huh?"

Ally laughed.

I laughed too, partly from relief.

Then I said, "I don't think sending notes is weird. I mean, I guess it's *rare*, but not weird." Violet Summers, Professor of Popularity, at your service.

"Phew!" Ally said, as if what I thought really mattered to her.

"It was nice," I said. "The note."

"Major phew!"

I smiled at her again. "Do you want my phone number? We could text."

"Yeah." She smiled bigger, obviously not realizing I was just trying to ward off more notes.

While we called each other to exchange numbers, my mom drove into the parking lot.

I said goodbye and got in the back seat, something Mom usually let me do only when a friend was coming along. She said it made her feel like even more of a chauffeur than she already was.

When Mom asked me who I'd been talking to, I was in such a good mood that I forgot to give my usual one-word response. Instead, I said, "Ally Ziegler, the girl who plays Dorothy. She's really nice."

"Oh!" Mom squealed, sounding shocked by my use of nine extra words. "It's terrific to make new friends!"

Mom didn't want me spending so much time with McKenzie. She really seemed to like McKenzie, but didn't like that she was the only kid I ever hung out with now. She never said that, but I could tell. It was similar to Mom letting me put ketchup on fries and burgers, but saying, "Really, Violet?"

when I put ketchup on teriyaki chicken and quesadillas and corn on the cob.

And I knew she was upset about McKenzie convincing me to quit Girl Scouts, because Mom had been our leader. She was always arranging field trips and searching for new craft projects for the troop. And cookie season! Besides making me ring about every doorbell within a half-mile radius of our house, Mom tried to sell cookies to anyone unfortunate enough to come by—even the UPS guy and the trash collectors.

I bet Mom missed being the boss of all those girls. Most of us would follow directions, like the good little Girl Scouts we were. But not McKenzie. When we made greeting cards with suns and smiley faces to cheer up people in the military, McKenzie drew a stick figure lying on the ground with bright red blood coming out of his stomach and the words, *I hope you kill the bad guys.* And when we sang Christmas carols and one Hanukkah song at the nursing home, McKenzie shouted for the old people to clap along to the beat, even during "Silent Night." The other moms said that was just plain wrong, but one of the old ladies said the Good Lord gave us hands for clapping, not finger-wagging.

McKenzie seemed to like Girl Scouts, until something bad happened between our mothers. It was the morning of our big camping trip. Everyone was supposed to meet at our house, but McKenzie didn't show up and her mom didn't answer her phone. (This was before we got our own cell phones, which improved our lives a quadrillion percent.) So Mom drove to McKenzie's house with me. We rang the doorbell and knocked. Then Mom peeked through the front window and told me to wait in the car.

As I watched from the front passenger seat, McKenzie opened the door to her house a little. Mom pushed it all the way open and stepped inside.

She quickly reeled back and McKenzie's mother came out, waving her arms and putting her face right next to Mom's. I didn't hear what she said, but it couldn't have been nice.

McKenzie had walked outside with a couple of old blankets and a pillow and a garbage bag of stuff that turned out to be clothes.

Mom ran after McKenzie, grabbed her stuff, and threw it in the car. "Get in!" Mom urged, and drove away, as fast as Grandpa Falls-Apart could go.

I didn't ask what happened. I still had no clue. It all seemed so awkward.

The camping trip wasn't even that fun, because Mom gave everyone a long lecture about kindness after McKenzie said some curse words to the girls who teased her about bringing old blankets instead of a sleeping bag. Mom seemed a lot madder about the teasing than the curse words.

Also, the whole cabin smelled like pee because Lena Markov had wet her sleeping bag the first night. Plus, I got stung by a wasp.

Thinking about those things in the car after rehearsal reminded me that McKenzie would be mad/sad if she found out Ally and I had traded phone numbers.

Then Mom asked, "Is she in seventh grade like you? She looks like she is."

I didn't say anything. It was strange hearing Mom happy about something two days after Dad had moved out.

"Is she in seventh grade?" Mom demanded.

I sighed. "Yes, Mom. Don't forget we're picking up McKenzie."

Mom sighed too, a totally exaggerated one. Then she said, "Yes, Violet," in an even wearier tone than I'd used.

I couldn't help laughing.

Mom told me a long time ago that I couldn't go over to McKenzie's house. It wasn't a big deal, because McKenzie never invited me over anyway. And I knew Mom liked bringing McKenzie to our house. For one thing, it probably made her feel like a better mother than McKenzie's mom. I told Mom once that McKenzie's mom let her ride her bike to the movies because she was part of the Free-Range Kids Movement, and Mom had answered, "Or the Lazy-Range Moms Movement." I'd responded that it was better than being in the Overbearing-Range Moms Movement. Then Mom had sighed for real.

For another thing, Mom could pump info from McKenzie that I wouldn't tell her. McKenzie wouldn't give away anything big, but she'd answer questions about little stuff, like what books we were supposed to read in English class.

McKenzie was waiting, as usual, on the sidewalk in front of her house. As she got in Grandpa Falls-Apart and buckled her seat belt, she said, "I'm sorry to hear about your marital separation."

"Thank you," Mom said, not sounding thankful.

"Where did Violet's dad go?" McKenzie asked. "Is he renting an apartment around here?"

Mom gazed in the rearview mirror at us. She was frowning.

I gazed right back at her and jutted my chin. It was about time Mom had to answer questions instead of asking them.

But she didn't say anything.

McKenzie said, "Mrs. Summers?"

I turned toward McKenzie. She was such a good friend. She probably didn't care where my dad was, but she knew that *I* cared and that I had a right to know. And she knew I was a wimp. So she stood up for me.

Finally, Mom cleared her throat and said, "I think Violet's father should be answering those questions."

Text to McKenzie: Thx for trying

McKenzie: YW

Mom stopped at a red light and turned back to us with a big, bright smile, like one of those peppy restaurant servers who you know, as soon as she leaves your table, starts complaining to the cook about the stupid customer who spent forever deciding between french fries or onion rings. "I'm making lasagna tonight!" Mom exclaimed as if she were making diamonds.

"You mean you're heating up frozen Costco lasagna," I grumbled. "Grandma makes homemade lasagna. And she and Aunt Amber are always baking homemade pies."

"Your grandma and Aunt Amber don't have preteen girls to drive around," Mom grumbled back.

Dad didn't bake pies, but he bought them every year for my birthday. Dad started the "Vi Day Is Pie Day" tradition when I turned ten. That morning, two pies sat on the kitchen table. In front of them was a note I ended up saving.

Happy birthday, Vi!
I give you permission to eat nothing but pie all day long.
          Love, Dad (and your reluctant mother)
P.S. There's 2 more pies in the fridge.
P.P.S. Save me some of the apple-pecan pie.
P.P.P.S. I couldn't resist eating a slice of the chocolate silk
P.P.P.P.S. And the blueberry.

Dad bought me pies on my eleventh and twelfth birthdays, too. I wondered what would happen when I turned thirteen. Mom would probably buy only one pie and let me have only one slice all day.

EIGHT

$\mathcal{I}$ loved Costco lasagna. But I didn't tell Mom that at dinner, since I'd just complained about it on the car ride home. She might have known though. She raised an eyebrow at me when I took a third helping, with ketchup. I wondered whether raising one eyebrow for a long time gave you a headache on only one side of your head.

After dinner, McKenzie and I watched music videos on my laptop in my room. They all seemed the same—beautiful people kissing or crying or making beautiful sad faces. We sang along, making up the lyrics we didn't already know.

Then we made popcorn with butter and honey and sat through an unromantic, unfunny romantic comedy starring a sweet, gorgeous actress and a cranky old guy. The best thing about the movie was joking around with McKenzie while we half watched it—pretending to puke when the couple kissed, calling the guy Creepy the Crank, and yelling at the actress, "You're too good for him!"

Once it ended, we changed into our pajamas. McKenzie wore her gray cotton nightgown that she called her sleepover uniform. The fabric had gotten thin, almost see-through, and there was a big stain near the bottom. I didn't know how McKenzie had stained it or why she kept wearing it. We never talked about that.

McKenzie got in the trundle bed, I turned out the light and lay in my bed, and we talked. We decided on the cutest guy at school, which ended up being a three-way tie, depending on whether you preferred big muscles (Gavin King), wavy black hair (Jorge Hernandez), or a cleft chin (Henry Tomaselli). I didn't mention Diego Ortiz. He didn't have big muscles or wavy hair or a cleft chin, but he had shiny eyes. Plus, he was tall and had a fantastic smile and beautiful teeth.

Then McKenzie said, "Okay, most stuck-up. I'm going with Ally."

I changed the subject. "How about best kind of pet?"

"Dog. Duh," McKenzie said.

"Yeah," I agreed.

"Favorite dessert?" McKenzie asked. "Hot fudge sundae for me. Pie for you. But what kind of pie?"

"Every kind." In the dark I pictured my grandmother slicing up five different homemade pies last Thanksgiving, saying, "All righty. Who wants what?" We'd called out, "I want it all!" and "Me first!" and "Pile it on!" Dad's relatives were as loud and almost as funny as him. Dad and I always took a sliver of each type of pie and a huge slice of Aunt Amber's caramel-apple pie. Had Dad moved in with Grandma and Grandpa in Fresno?

"Are you awake?" McKenzie asked.

"Just trying to figure out my favorite type of pie. I like every kind except mincemeat and sweet potato pie. It should be illegal to call those things pie!"

McKenzie laughed. "Okay. How about things we wouldn't do even for a million dollars?"

"We answered that one before," I said. "Kill someone nice, eat poop, and . . ."

"Give someone more than a million dollars," McKenzie said. "Now I remember."

While I was trying to think of other interesting questions

and fighting off sleep, McKenzie said, "It's a mystery."

"What's a mystery?" I asked.

"Why I thought I wanted to be in *The Wizard of Oz*. It's a play for little kids. What twelve-year-old wants to sing about witches and wizards and wear silly costumes?"

McKenzie did, that's who. She'd wanted to sing about a rainbow and wear a cute dress and sparkly red shoes. I didn't say that, or anything else.

"We're at school all day. Why would we stay there any later than we have to?" she said.

Why? The reason came to me as I lay still in bed. Because after-school rehearsals beat McKenzie staying at home with her mother, who had yelled into my mom's face, or me staying at home with my fake-cheery mom, with no father for either one of us.

"We should quit," McKenzie said.

I kept quiet, grateful for the dark.

"We should do it now so Goldstein has time to recast our parts. If I had any idea we'd get such bad ones, I never would have tried out in the first place."

But *we* didn't get bad parts. *She* got a bad part. I stared at the nothingness above me. There was more to the play than avoiding home. I wanted to be in the auditorium with the other people who stayed after school. Diego made me laugh. Mr. Goldstein saw something in me that no one else ever had. Ally saw something in me too, something different from what Mr. Goldstein saw, something good enough to write me a nice note and track down my locker to deliver it. For some reason, she liked me. I wasn't supposed to like *her*, but I did.

This Girl Scout song went: *Make new friends, but keep the old. One is silver and the other gold.* I had McKenzie, but why couldn't I have Ally too? According to the song, old gold friend McKenzie > new silver friend Ally. But who was better if the old friend said you sang like a kitten and the new friend said you were really talented?

"We need to quit," McKenzie said.

That's what she'd said about Girl Scouts, and I'd gone right along. But sometimes I wished I hadn't. Mom had planned for the troop to try to earn robotics badges, which meant learning how to code. Plus, she'd been arranging a boat trip to Catalina Island.

Maybe even worse, Mom had taken the news hard. When

I'd told her I was quitting Scouts, her face got all stiff like the Botoxed ladies in the rich areas of Orange County. After about a quadrillion years, Mom had said in a voice as stiff as her face, "It's your decision, Violet."

Mom didn't have anything to do with the play, so she wouldn't care as much about that. But I would. A lot.

I told McKenzie, "I never thought about quitting."

"Think about it now, Violet," McKenzie said. "You'll have to wear a dorky, furry costume. And we'll have to watch Goldstein fawn over Ally at every rehearsal, which will make her even more conceited."

Actually, Mr. Goldstein hadn't fawned over Ally since her first audition. He'd told her she needed to play Dorothy with more vim—whatever that was—and find her hard edge. Diego had joked that she should find the hard edge fast, before anyone hurt themselves on it.

"I'll email Goldstein right now and tell him we're quitting," McKenzie went on. "I'll tell him we can't, like, connect with our characters. He loves that artsy psychology talk. Ugh. That's another reason for quitting: not having to hear Goldstein go on about everything's secret inner meaning."

But sometimes I liked thinking about secret inner meanings.

"So, turn your laptop on, Violet. I'll email him and sign it from both of us."

I sat up in my bed but stayed there.

McKenzie got out of the trundle bed, turned on the flashlight on her phone, and pointed it at me. "Well?" She stared at me hard.

I turned away from her and said to my wall, just loud enough for McKenzie to hear, "I'm not quitting the play."

"What?" McKenzie said.

I knew she'd heard me, so I didn't answer.

"Fine!" she fumed. "I'll quit and you can stay in the stupid play. But don't complain about it and expect any sympathy from me."

"Okay," I said. Though things weren't okay, and we both knew it.

NINE

Hi Dad,

I hope you're all right, because you didn't answer my email from over a week ago. I'm not trying to be a nag. I know you don't like nags. I just worry about you.

Will you come to my play, please? It's *The Wizard of Oz*, and I play the Lion, which is a big part.

Remember Bonzo's? That barbecue place we used to go to? It serves those giant slabs of fatty ribs and extra creamy coleslaw and rolls that practically drip butter. I have a huge craving for it. I know Mom won't take me. Remember she always said she preferred quality over quantity and there was too much grease in the food, but you always said she should live a little? Next time you're in town, maybe we can go there together? Or somewhere else. Maybe somewhere Mom likes too. We like Italian food, all three of us. We could go to Roma's together, just like old times when we shared the Family Special. Let's live a little. ☺

Love,
Vi

Dear Mr. Pagano,

I have been working very hard on our school play, because I would like to make everyone at our school proud, especially you. After rehearsals, I work on memorizing my lines. So I haven't had time for other important things, like reading, which explains my grade on the test about *The Scarlet Pimpernel*. Can you please skip that test for me in the grading chart?

Sincerely,
Violet Summers

Dear Violet,

No.

Sincerely,
Mr. Pagano

Text to McKenzie: I should have read *Scarlet Pimple Nail*—Autocorrect haha—or at least the SparkNotes. Bombed the test. I told my mom everyone bombed it, so plz back me up if she asks

Dear Ms. Merriweather,

I have been working very hard on our school play, because I would like to make everyone at our school proud, especially you. After rehearsals, I work on memorizing my lines. So I haven't had time for other important things, like math homework, which explains why I haven't turned it in this week. Can you please skip the homework this week in the grading chart?

Sincerely,

Violet Summers

Dear Violet Summers,

Please come to my room at lunchtime.

Ms. Merriweather

When the lunch bell rang, I made my way so slowly to Ms. Merriweather's class. It was more like shuffling than walking.

Then I stood near Ms. Merriweather's door, which was open at about a fifteen-degree angle. My arms were crossed, and my brain was knotted up in thoughts. I'd told my teachers the truth about spending my time rehearsing *The Wizard of Oz* instead of doing homework. They obviously didn't appreciate my honesty. They also obviously didn't support the arts.

I didn't care much about my grades, considering everything going on these days. But my mom cared—and I cared about her not taking my phone away. My dad didn't care about grades like Mom did. Maybe he didn't care at all anymore.

"Come on in, Violet," Ms. Merriweather said. She didn't sound mad, but that might have just been wishful thinking.

I walked in.

Ms. Merriweather motioned me closer and told me to sit down. So I sat on a chair a few inches from her, which was the first time in middle school I'd ever sat so close to a teacher. I hoped it would be the last.

"Violet, you're still not paying attention in class. And you didn't do your homework."

I bit my lip.

"Yet you only missed one question on the math test yesterday. You obviously know your stuff." Ms. Merriweather smiled at me. "You're an interesting girl. You never speak up, but I have a feeling you're on top of everything I'm teaching you. Am I right?"

I stopped biting my lip and let a smile escape.

"You need more of a challenge," Ms. Merriweather said. "From now on, you only have to do every other math problem for the homework."

You'd think a math teacher would be able to calculate that doing only half the homework was not more of a challenge. I didn't correct her though, because her mistake meant less homework for me. So instead I said, "Thank you, Ms. Merri-weather."

She nodded quickly. "If I'm explaining something to the class and you already know it, you may ignore me."

I get to ignore the teacher! I shouted in my head.

"I'll give you supplemental assignments to work on."

I stopped smiling. Being singled out in math class would probably earn me a horrible nickname like Weird Violet or The Calculator. Math talent was the worst thing to be recognized for. It was even dorkier than science talent, because that could be used to make stink bombs.

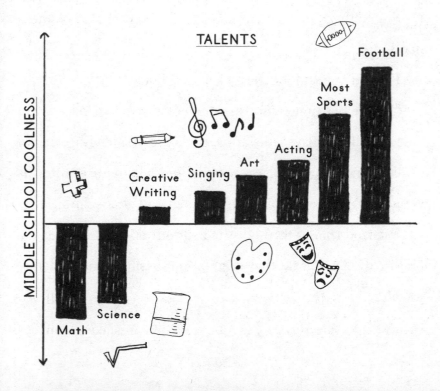

"You won't be the only one," Ms. Merriweather said as if reading my mind. "One of your classmates is also doing supplemental work."

"Who?" I asked.

She shuffled through some papers on her desk. "I can't say. The other student is self-conscious about her—his or her, I mean—exceptional math talent. But I believe math skills are something to be proud of. Don't you?"

I shrugged. "You might as well keep my identity a secret too."

Ms. Merriweather pursed her magenta lips.

"Please, Ms. Merriweather."

She sighed and said, "All right." Then she gave me a handout.

I stared at it. It looked thick and difficult.

"There's a homework assignment every few pages. Let me know if you have questions, if it's too challenging, or not challenging enough. Please come in and talk to me as often as you'd like. I'm here most days at lunch and after school."

I started leafing through the handout. Math history facts. Math trivia. A puzzle that seemed impossible, but probably wasn't.

"Once you turn in these assignments, I'll give you more, all right?"

The next page showed a timeline graph! Then a picto-graph! Then some charts I'd never seen before. A pyramid chart? What in the world was that?

"All right, Violet?"

Something called a sunburst chart! Whoa!

"All right, Violet?" Ms. Merriweather said loudly.

I forced my gaze from the handout. "It's one hundred per-cent all right, Ms. Merriweather!"

TEN

VIOLET SUMMERS
7TH GRADE MATH

MS. MERRIWEATHER, PERIOD I

Supplemental Homework: Five Interesting Facts About Pi

1. It's easy to memorize the first eight digits of pi.
Just count the number of letters in each word of:

"May I have a large container of coffee?"
  3 1 4 1 5   9   2   6

2. Albert Einstein was born on Pi Day (March 14 or 3/14).

3. The mirror image of 314 (pi) is PIE.

4. A guy in India is in the *Guinness Book of World Records* for memorizing the first 70,000 digits of pi. It took him more than 17 hours to recite all the digits.

5. If a cylinder has a radius of Z and a height of A, the formula for the cylinder's volume is Pi x Z x Z x A.

We'd spent the past two weeks of rehearsal working on blocking, which meant learning where to move onstage. Mr. Goldstein said our bodies were instruments. Diego joked that his body felt like a battered drum.

I'd practiced my big solo in the shower a quadrillion times. The repetition of singing my "Courage" song became as relaxing as yoga, or how yoga is supposed to make you feel. We had to do it in P.E. class last year, and I spent the whole period making sure I didn't fall asleep or fart.

The only thing I did more than rehearse the song was check my email—and voicemail and missed calls and text messages. But there was nothing from my dad.

I was pretty sure he hadn't died or anything. I'd asked Mom, "You'd find out if Dad died, right? And you'd tell me?"

She'd looked at me like I was an orphaned kitten. "I'd find out and you'd find out," she said. "Your dad isn't dead. He's just . . ." She'd furled her eyebrows, like she was thinking Dad was a kitten orphaner. Then she looked away for a bit.

When she turned back to me, her face had calmed down, but her hand was balled into a fist. She said, "Your dad is alive. He's fine."

That didn't give me much relief. Because if he was fine, why was he ignoring me?

There was one benefit of Dad disappearing: I had more important things to worry about today at rehearsal than my big moment, singing my solo in front of everyone. Actually, big *moments*, plural, because a moment is approximately a second, and my song lasted about a minute and a half, which meant approximately ninety seconds, a.k.a. moments.

So anyway, I was pretty calm when I sang "If I Only Had the Nerve" in front of Mr. Goldstein and the cast.

After I finished, Ally clapped and said, "Nailed it, Violet!"

Mr. Goldstein nodded at me and said, "You have natural talent."

I beamed on center stage, though I couldn't help thinking I got my "natural talent" from practicing so hard at home.

Then Diego said, "That's nothing. I have *supernatural* talent." He tied the sleeves of his sweatshirt around his neck so it looked like a cape, spread his arms out like they were wings, and jumped off the stage.

Everyone laughed, even Mr. Goldstein.

I'd worked in plenty of groups before. During the first week of school, I'd had to do a skit about the American

Revolution with three other kids in my history class. James M. kept complaining about how cheesy the skit was, Lyla Lopez refused to wear a wig, everyone fought over who got to play George Washington, and Anna Markel kept shrieking that we idiots would destroy her perfect grade point average. We ended up getting a B-plus, but I hated every minute of the project, except for eating the homemade cherry pie Anna Markel brought in for extra credit.

Play rehearsals were different than an assigned skit, because we wanted to be there. We had spent hours after school auditioning for the chance to stay after school many more hours, plus a few Saturdays. We pulled for one another to make the play as good as possible.

The more choice you had in doing something, the more you cooperated.

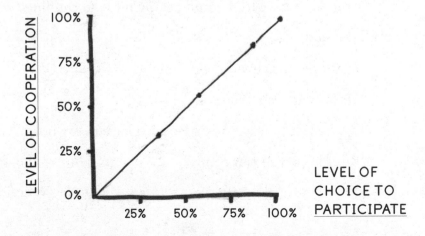

As I walked down the stage steps at the end of rehearsal, Ally said behind me, "I can't believe we're supposed to have everything memorized so soon."

"I know!" I said, waiting for her at the bottom of the stairs. "I mean, I *don't* know. I don't know a lot of my lines."

"Maybe we could practice during lunchtime," Ally said.

I didn't say anything back. I couldn't leave McKenzie alone in the school cafeteria while I rehearsed with her worst enemy!

"Or do you want to come over tomorrow after rehearsal? We could eat dinner and then run lines."

I stared at Ally. Was she inviting me to her house? On a Friday night? Didn't she have a bunch of better offers? The invite must have been a spur-of-the-moment thing. She was probably already regretting it.

"You don't have to. I could get my mom to run lines with me," she said.

Okay. She *was* already regretting it.

"Or my dad," she said.

To save face, to save Ally's face, I'd have to say no.

"But I hope you can come."

"No. Oh. I mean, yes. Yes, that would be fun. Useful, I mean. Fun, too. Thanks."

Ally nodded.

If McKenzie found out about me going to Ally's house, she'd be so upset. She'd never understand. Unless I told her it was for the sake of the play. Or that Mr. Goldstein forced us to practice together. Or . . . Or . . .

"Do you?" Ally asked.

"Do I what?"

"Do you need to check with your parents?"

My mom would be thrilled I'd made a new friend, a friend besides McKenzie. And I couldn't check with my dad even if I wanted to. Which I did.

I said, "I'm sure it'll be fine."

"Great. My mom can drive us to my house after rehearsal tomorrow."

"Don't you have to ask her first?" I said.

Ally smiled. "I already did."

ELEVEN

That night I dreamed I was at Ally's house, an enormous white mansion with grand, cylindrical columns in front and shiny marble floors inside. I sat at a long, oval table piled with platters of steak, lobster, and doughnuts. Then Ally screamed at me, "Who do you think you are, sitting at my dining room table! I invited you here to wash dishes with the other servants. Get up, Violet! Get up!"

I opened my eyes and heard Mom calling, "Get up, Violet! Get up! You'll be late for school!"

I rubbed my eyes. Even my dreams were dorky. That enormous white mansion I'd dreamed up was the White House. And who has platters of doughnuts at the dinner table? Though if I were the president, I'd order my staff to serve doughnuts and pie every night.

As Mom left my room, she told me to hurry and get dressed.

It was hard to choose what to wear while Mom kept saying "Come on" and "What are you doing in there?" etc. every two seconds. All she did was ruin my concentration and slow me down.

If I'd known Ally was going to invite me over, I wouldn't have worn my favorite outfit two days before. (My only pair of expensive jeans, which Mom and Dad had given me for my birthday, and a horizontally striped sweater that made me look not completely flat-chested.) I decided to wear my expensive jeans again and hoped no one would notice.

But choosing a sweater was harder. People would know if I wore the same one twice in one week. McKenzie did it a lot, but she only had four sweaters, including one that barely fit. I never said anything, but I noticed. So I vetoed my favorite sweater due to recent wear. And I couldn't wear my second favorite, because it was dirty. My third favorite sweater was my favorite color—pink. But the first day I wore it, McKenzie had said, "That sweater sure is bright."

I finally decided to wear my fourth favorite sweater, a brown wool one that Mom said brought out my dark eyes. After putting it on, I realized its left sleeve was stained.

I was trying to decide what my fifth favorite sweater was

when my mom yelled, "Violet, you have precisely sixty seconds before I take your phone away for a week!"

So I put on my "sure-is-bright" pink sweater and expensive jeans and cute-but-too-tight boots, hurried out of my room, and said, "I'm ready."

"What about breakfast?" Mom asked. "I made scrambled eggs."

"Thanks. I'll eat in the car." I plopped some ketchup on the eggs, sandwiched them between two slices of bread, grabbed a paper towel, my phone, and backpack, and headed out of the house.

Mom followed me, lecturing me about going to bed earlier and setting my alarm and acting responsible, blah blah blah.

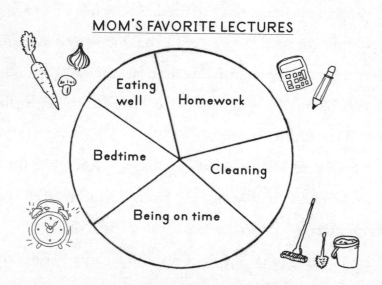

MOM'S FAVORITE LECTURES

Eating well

Homework

Bedtime

Cleaning

Being on time

As I fastened my seat belt and put my egg sandwich on my lap, Mom said, "Don't make a habit of eating in the car. I have to keep it pristine. I want my clients thinking Grandpa Falls-Apart is a cool classic car instead of a junky old heap."

She turned the key in the ignition.

The car sputtered.

She turned the key again. Grandpa Falls-Apart made a weak, weary whine.

The third time, the car did nothing.

Mom rested her head on the steering wheel and said, "Great. Just great."

"What's wrong?" I asked.

I meant what was wrong with the car, but Mom said, "Everything," and a tear fell halfway down her cheek. She wiped it away roughly, like she was mad at it for daring to wet her face.

Then she sighed and straightened her head and said, "Hopefully, only the battery. But who knows? This car is older than you are. I'll walk you to school."

"It's cold and I'll be late," I said. Plus, my feet were already achy in my tight boots. I didn't tell Mom that, because they were my cutest footwear and changing out of them would make me even later.

"I'll write you a tardy note."

"Too bad Dad's not here. He could have drove me."

"Ha," Mom said, but it wasn't a laughing *ha*.

I crossed my arms. "What's that supposed to mean?"

"There's a difference between could have and would have," she said.

I kept my arms crossed and didn't say anything.

"Well, your dad's not here, so let's go," Mom said.

I opened the car door and hurried out, forgetting about the scrambled egg sandwich on my lap. It fell and became unsandwiched on the way down, leaving red streaks and yellow lumps all over the floor mat.

"Great. Just great," Mom said again.

She got out of the car as I picked up the mess and dumped it in the trash can.

"Let's go," Mom said. "I'll clean up the rest later."

I wiped my hands with the paper towel. "I'm twelve. I can walk to school by myself."

"And I suppose your history project will walk itself to school too."

"Oh. I forgot."

"That's why I made you put it in the car last night." Mom opened the trunk.

I peered down at my stupid California Gold Rush scene I'd started and finished last night, taping and gluing old toys and household junk onto foam board left over from last year's science fair project. My stupid Lego people were dwarfed by my stupid plastic My Little Pony figurines, which were dwarfed by the stupid stagecoach I'd made from chopsticks, toothbrushes, and toilet paper. I'd tried to create a lake from aluminum foil, but it just looked like aluminum foil. The whole project turned out awful, but it had taken me less than an hour while watching TV and would probably earn me at least a B-minus. It was too bulky to carry 1.3 miles to school by myself.

As Mom peered into the trunk and picked at her cuticle, I asked her, "Can you just drop this stupid thing off at school once the car is fixed?"

"What period do you have history?"

"Second."

"Then no. Grandpa Falls-Apart might not be fixed by then. I'll help you carry it to school."

"Maybe Dad can come and drive me," I said, staring down at the trunk again.

Mom didn't respond.

"Mom?"

"Fine." She sounded anything but fine. And her cuticle had torn, leaving a spot of blood on her ring finger. "Call him," she said.

I stared at the open trunk again. Even when he lived here, Dad didn't drive me to school. He worked late at whatever bar or restaurant he was assistant managing or waitering or bartending at, then slept until eleven or noon. In February, Mom had sprained her ankle and couldn't drive for a week. I had to walk to school, even that morning it rained.

"Let's just go," I said.

Mom and I hauled out my stupid project, and we started walking. My feet already hurt from the tight boots.

"I hope no one I know sees me like this," I said.

"I hope they do and offer you a ride," Mom said. "Although I'm sure everyone's left for school by now. Unlike you, who slept late and then dawdled in your bedroom and then spilled the eggs I made all over my car."

I hadn't heard her this grumpy since Dad lived with us.

I'd forgotten how mad she could sound. She'd blamed her sprained ankle on Dad because she'd tripped over his shoes in the hallway. He'd told her she should have watched her step and to stop trying to make everything his fault. Even though it had meant walking to school in the rain, I had felt kind of relieved to get away from their arguing.

That morning it had been raining hard—not just cats and dogs, but bobcats and wolves. I had an umbrella, but I didn't own a raincoat. You don't need one in Orange County, because it hardly ever rains, and everyone rides in cars anyway. Except for me that day. I stared at the ground, out of misery and the need to avoid puddles, which are only fun to splash in when you don't have to worry about spending all day in school wearing soggy shoes and wet jeans. I wished for a raincoat. I wished my mom's ankle wasn't sprained. I wished my dad had gotten out of bed and driven me to school. None of my wishes came true. Not exactly.

I was only about two blocks from our house that morning when I heard a car pull up beside me. Before I could say "Stranger Danger," Mom had shouted from the driver's seat, "Violet, get in!" So I'd hurried into Grandpa Falls-Apart.

Then Mom had driven in silence. At every stop sign, when

Mom had to step on the brake and then the gas pedal, her face winced in pain.

Dad really should have apologized for leaving his shoes out. And also for not driving me that morning.

I looked at Mom now, walking beside me, and said, "I'm sorry for waking up so late."

After a pause, Mom said softly, "It's okay. I'm mostly upset about the car."

"And I shouldn't have done my stupid history project at the last minute."

"Yeah, well, I wouldn't mind so much if it were smaller, like a stupid shoebox diorama." She laughed.

I laughed too.

Then to cheer her up more and because I had to tell her anyway, I said, "Can I go to Ally Ziegler's house today after rehearsal? Her parents can drive both ways."

"Ally Ziegler?" Mom asked.

"The girl you saw me talking to after rehearsal."

"Dorothy!" Mom's face lit up, like she was overjoyed. "Sure. Call or text me when you get there, okay?"

"Okay," I said. "Thanks. Thanks a lot, Mom."

TWELVE

SURPRISING THINGS ABOUT ALLY

Her house is only about 1,200 square feet and pretty messy.

She has twin little sisters.

Ally's parents are old, like at least fifty.

Ally's sisters and parents are tall and have pretty blue eyes like Ally, but their skin color doesn't match hers.

- Ally always looks like she just came out of a tanning salon.

- The rest of the family is white.

- They aren't just white. They're spent-their-lives-in-a-cave, have-to-put-on-sunblock-every-forty-five-minutes white.

At dinner Ally did a hilarious imitation of our French teacher, saying, "Bone shure, cheeldren," and fluttering her hands like a flock of birds.

When the twins told knock-knock jokes, Ally's parents gave them adoring looks.

- The knock-knock jokes were really dumb.

  For example: "Knock, knock."
  "Who's there?"
  "Ya."
  "Ya who?"
  "I'm excited to see you too."

Ally's parents also gave each other adoring looks.

Dinner at Ally's house was about 250% louder than dinner at mine.

- McKenzie's house noise is probably in the middle. She said she and her mom eat while watching *Wheel of Fortune*.

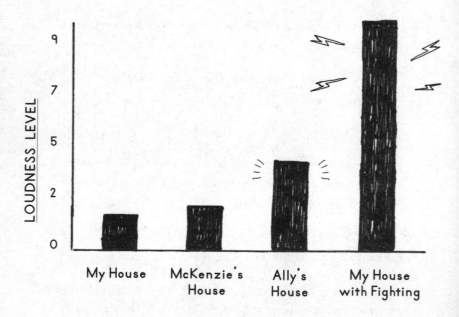

It wasn't fair that Ally was beautiful and popular and a great singer *and* funny *and* had two nice, happy parents. Except her sisters were annoying. Sometimes I wished I had a sister or brother, but that night I was grateful I didn't.

After Ally and I cleared the dinner table, we went to her bedroom. It was even tinier than mine, barely fitting a twin bed, a tall, narrow dresser with clothes piled on top, and a small closet. It was cute, though, with butter yellow walls and a thick comforter with a pink-and-yellow daisy print on her bed.

"Nice room," I said.

"Thanks. I like it, even though it doesn't fit all my stuff." She gestured to her dresser. "I get tons of hand-me-down clothes from my mom's boss's daughter. My sisters' room is bigger, but they have to share."

I wondered whether my mom liked having her own room now that my dad had moved out.

I frowned. Maybe she loved it.

Ally and I sat facing each other on her bed, with our scripts on our legs. Ally kept her sneakers on, so I kept my boots on. My feet were dying of pain. But the embarrassment of possibly stinking up Ally's bedroom with smelly feet would make my heart die of pain, which was worse.

We started with Ally cuing me for the Lion scenes. I knew about 80 percent of my lines.

Then I cued Ally. She had about three times more lines than me, but she'd barely memorized anything. Her nose kept wrinkling up as she tried to remember her lines. Even with a wrinkled-up nose, Ally looked beautiful. Life is so unfair. If I wrinkled my nose, I'd just look weird.

I was glad McKenzie couldn't see me now. I knew I shouldn't be here, with her worst enemy. But I was. And I was having fun.

After a few minutes, Ally turned her script upside down, covered her face in her hands, and said, "I'll never, ever remember all this! If there were an understudy to do my part, I'd quit right now."

I looked away. McKenzie had wanted to play Dorothy so badly. If she ever found out what Ally just said, she'd call her a drama queen. She'd say, *How dare Ally take the best part in the play and then act like it's such a burden! She has everything and now she wants sympathy, too.* And she'd be right.

I narrowed my eyes and turned toward Ally.

112

Oh no. She was crying. It was a delicate cry. She barely made a sound, but tears dripped down to her chin.

I didn't know what to say, so I just said, "Ally?" It came out like a question.

"Sorry," she murmured. "You must think I'm a spoiled, attention-seeking baby."

"I don't," I said, even though I sort of had been thinking that.

She moved her hands away from her face. The tears trickled slowly now. "I don't know how I can learn my part. There are so many lines. It's too much. I'm not smart like you."

"Me?"

"It takes me forever to memorize stuff. I'll mess up the play, and everyone in the cast and my parents will be so upset. Except the mean people at school who love when other kids mess up."

"They're just jealous," I said. I couldn't help picturing McKenzie when I said it.

"They shouldn't be." Ally wiped the last tears from her cheeks. "And they shouldn't act so mean."

I bit my lip. Was McKenzie mean? Was I?

"Listen," I said. "You should study the script extra hard, to show the jealous people that you deserve the part."

Ally slowly nodded. "Yeah." But then one more tear dripped down her cheek. "I'm also scared that if I screw up, some people will say, 'Dorothy was never supposed to have dark skin.'"

I didn't know how to respond. I hadn't thought about what color Dorothy's skin was or what color it should be. I'd figured Ally was the right person to play Dorothy because she sang "Somewhere over the Rainbow" the best and acted so well.

"Hey, thanks for listening, Violet." Ally's sweet voice broke into my thoughts.

"I feel bad," I said.

"You feel bad too?" Ally asked.

"I mean I feel bad you have to worry about people saying bad stuff."

"Thanks. I should stop feeling sorry for myself."

I tried to think of something else to say. I wasn't used to comforting people. Plus, it was hard to concentrate while my feet were throbbing. Finally, I just said, "Let's continue where we left off," which sounded like a teacher phrase.

Someone knocked on Ally's door, even though it was part-way open.

"What?" Ally said in the same irritated tone I used when my mom knocked on my door.

The door swung open. Ally's parents stood in the door-way, so close to each other they could have been a two-headed person.

"How are you girls doing?" Ally's mom asked. She and Ally's dad wore identically dorky, eager smiles.

"Fine," Ally said.

"We have Oreos if you want. Double Stuf. They're in the kitchen," her dad said.

Ally sighed as if he'd just told her celery was in the kitchen. "We're trying to work here."

After her parents left, Ally said, "They're always checking up on me."

"My mom does that too," I said.

"My dad especially. He hovers over me, like he doesn't trust me to take care of myself."

My dad trusted me. Why wouldn't he? I never did any-thing bad.

Maybe if I did something bad, my dad would come home.

It would have to be very bad, so bad my mom couldn't handle it herself.

"I wish they didn't butt in like that," Ally said.

I leaned toward her. "Why don't your parents trust you? Did you do something really bad?"

"*I* didn't," she said. "Their daughter did."

"One of your little sisters?"

"Huh? Oh." Ally shook her head. "Long story."

"Sorry."

"Not your fault." Ally shrugged, but she was frowning.

"It's just that my dad is, like, the opposite of your dad. He moved out a few weeks ago." Seventeen days ago, to be precise. "I haven't heard from him, so I was wondering how to get him to act more like *your* dad."

Ally set down her script again. "Violet, I'm so sorry."

I was no longer in charge, no longer the line cue-er or comforter or advice giver. I was just my ordinary self again. Back to clueless, pathetic Violet.

"It's not *your* fault your dad's acting like that," Ally continued.

"I know." I tried to shrug but couldn't even do a fake one. "It's my mom's fault for nagging him too much."

"He could still call you, right? Or pick you up from school."

"Look, it hasn't actually been a *few* weeks. It's only been a *couple* of weeks, just two weeks plus a few days."

Ally stared at me like I was a real estate agent trying to explain away mold damage on a house.

"He might be out of town. And maybe he lost my cell number."

Ally raised her eyebrows. "Couldn't he email you? Your dad shouldn't, like, ghost you."

I put down my script and crossed my arms. "He didn't *ghost* me. You don't even know him. Just because your parents totally dote on you all the—"

Ally interrupted me. "You don't know my parents either. You have no idea."

"Oh, please." I rolled my eyes. "I saw them at dinner. *And* they acted all lovey-dovey in your doorway, like . . . like Batman and Robin, or Hansel and Gretel."

"What?" Ally glared at me. "Isn't Batman Robin's guardian? And Hansel and Gretel are brother and sister. They're not lovey-dovey."

"Whatever." I glared back at her. "Can your parents

drive me home now? Or should I call my mom for a ride?"

"You can stay," Ally said. But her arms were crossed now too.

I crossed my arms tighter. "I want to go."

π

My mother opened the front door about a tenth of a second after I knocked, as if she'd been waiting for me with her hand on the doorknob. She bombarded me with questions right away: "How was it? Did you have fun? You had dinner there, right?"

I hurried past her and threw my backpack on the couch, which I knew she hated because she was a freaky neat freak, but I didn't care. "Where's Dad?" I asked loudly.

Mom frowned. "Did something happen at Ally's house?"

"Don't change the subject!" I shouted.

"Violet!" Mom snapped.

I took a deep breath and said very slowly, "Where. Is. My. Father."

Mom stared at me, wide-eyed.

"I'd like to know why he hasn't answered my emails."

Mom's eyes got wider. "You emailed him?"

"Is he mad at me because I acted bratty when he told me he was leaving?" I plopped onto the couch.

"No, Violet." Mom sat next to me and took a deep breath like I had done. "None of your father's actions are your fault. Not his leaving, not his . . . It has nothing to do with you."

I hated how her voice got all pitying, as if I were a starving orphan, even though I was much better off than a starving orphan, and even better off than McKenzie, whose dad was dead and who'd been cast as a monkey in the school play and whose very best friend in the world had totally betrayed her tonight.

"You emailed him?" Mom asked again, but not in a shocked way this time. She asked it like my emailing Dad was the saddest thing she'd ever heard, confirming her opinion that I was as pathetic as a starving orphan. She scooted closer to me on the couch. "When did you email him?"

"Stop asking questions!" I screamed. "Not until you answer mine!"

"Oh, Violet," Mom said, still not telling me anything about Dad.

I stood and hurried upstairs, my aching feet throbbing on each step.

Once I made it into my room, I closed my door and sat with my back against it to keep my mom out. Then I took off my boots and rubbed my feet. My feet didn't stink after all. At least I couldn't smell them. But maybe that's like a fart situation, where your own never smell as bad as other people's.

I shouldn't have told my mom I'd emailed Dad. I shouldn't have told her anything. Not when she refused to tell me the one thing I needed to know. And I shouldn't have told Ally about Dad or gone to her house in the first place behind McKenzie's back.

Ally acted like my dad was the worst, but she didn't know anything about him, about the fun we had together. A few times last summer when Mom was holding open houses, Dad and I had snuck into the swimming pool of the Shoreham Arms, a giant apartment complex nearby. The pool was always crowded, but it was amazing on hot days. We'd jump into the water, doing cannonballs, and then sit on ratty lounge chairs to play poker. Mom had told Dad that trespassing set a bad example for me. Plus, she got mad when I came back sunburned.

She didn't understand Dad either.

I turned my phone back on. McKenzie had texted three separate times:

5:03 p.m.: Wanna see a movie?

6:15 p.m.: Where R U?

6:41 p.m.: R U ok?

I texted her back:

Fell asleep. Sorry. Dumb rehearsals are so tiring. Ally is so annoying. Movie tomorrow?

And then, because maybe I really was the most pathetic person in the world, I checked my email again.

Nothing from my dad.

Of course not.

THIRTEEN

MATH PROBLEMS

1. If x = the lucky girl who won a leading role in the school play, and y = the 40 disappointed girls who tried out for the play but didn't get the leading role, then what is the ratio of x to y?

2. How many times more obligated is x to learn her lines than someone in the y group?

3. If x doesn't learn her lines, should she feel 40 times guiltier than anyone else?

ANSWER KEY

1. 1 to 40.

2. 40 times more obligated.

3. Definitely.

I'd gotten through rehearsals on Monday and Tuesday without saying one word to Ally, except in character as the

Lion. I wished I'd been cast as the Wicked Witch so I could yell at her.

But after Tuesday's rehearsal, as I hurried through the auditorium to get out of there as quick as possible, while pretending not to care that Ally was sitting in an aisle seat right next to Diego and probably flirting with him, my backpack slipped down a little and hit Ally's arm.

"Sorry," I blurted out.

I was sorry as soon as I said it. I didn't want Ally to think I was apologizing for how I'd acted at her house, or for anything else. So I added, "But your arm was dangling in the aisle."

"Blame the victim, why don't you?" Diego said with a laugh.

Ally and I glared at him. Usually he was funny, but not that time. He didn't even look very cute.

I hurried out of the auditorium, into the parking lot, and into Grandpa Falls-Apart.

Mom began interrogating me. *How was rehearsal? How did school go? How was lunch?*

"Fine. Fine. Fine," I said through gritted teeth. Though I smiled inside on the third "fine" when I thought about lunch. McKenzie and I had acted super silly, using carrot sticks and raisins to make stick figures we named Sammy Squarehead and Black-eyed Bob. We reassured them that even though they were made of food, they wouldn't be eaten. No one ever actually ate carrot sticks or raisins.

Grandpa Falls-Apart groaned mysteriously through the school parking lot.

Mom groaned too. "Oh no."

But we made it out of the lot and down the street with no more groans from the car or my mother.

"Violet," Mom said. "Do you want to help me get my new listing ready for the open house?"

"No," I said.

"It's a beautiful house. And I'll be baking cookies and arranging fresh flowers. Tempted?"

"No. I'd only be tempted by baking pies."

"Remember when we did that for the townhouse listing in Fullerton?" Mom shook her head. "Someone got peach filling on the ivory couch. And there were pie crumbs in every room. How about coming with me to the open house on Sunday?"

"No," I said as Grandpa Falls-Apart sputtered up our driveway.

"Are you sure things are fine?" Mom asked.

"No," I said. "I mean, yes. They're fine. Everything's fine."

She turned off the ignition. "Do you—"

"Mom!" I interrupted. "I'll tell you if school or rehearsal or lunch or anything else isn't fine!" I flung open the car door. "And you'll be the first to know if I ever become interested in real estate, which I'm not! So you don't need to ask!" I got out of the car and slammed the door shut.

Then I rushed into the house, right to my room, and slammed my bedroom door shut too. I sat on my bed with my laptop and checked my email for the quadrillionth time, so I could make my awful day even worse.

O.M.G! Dad emailed me!

Hello, Violet. I'm sorry I didn't respond sooner. I've been traveling a lot.

I'm very proud that you have a big part in *The Wizard of Oz*. I know you'll do a wonderful job. Unfortunately, I doubt I'll get to come to your play. I will be out of town that week.

Please understand that the reasons behind my leaving have nothing to do with you. Also, the reasons I haven't been in touch the last few weeks have nothing to do with you and everything to do with me.

I love you very much.

Love,
Dad

I knew he'd write me back!

I read the email again, nodding at my laptop as if my dad were on the other side of the screen. He said he loved me very much! He said he was proud of me!

I read it again. It was a perfect email. Okay, he couldn't come to my play. And he hadn't asked to see me, hadn't told me he'd call. But, still.

I read it again. *Couldn't* come to my play or *wouldn't* come to my play?

"Violet! Dinner!" Mom yelled from the kitchen.

"Coming!" I yelled back. But then I read Dad's email three

more times. All my work memorizing lines came in handy, because I could recite my father's email by heart.

Dinner was heated-up canned pea soup and frozen fish sticks with lots of ketchup. Maybe if Mom were a good cook like my grandmother and Aunt Amber, who made delicious food every Thanksgiving, Dad would have liked being home more. Or if Mom treated our house like one of her open houses, making sure every room smelled perfect, Dad would want to live here.

At dinner I acted like my usual self, giving one-word answers to Mom's questions and mostly ignoring her chatter about new trends in paint colors, flooring versus carpeting, and other unfascinating topics.

But I faked my poutiness tonight. Every time I thought about Dad's email, especially his *I love you very much,* I had to fight off a huge smile.

FOURTEEN

Dear Dad,

It was great getting your email!

I'm sorry you can't come to *The Wizard of Oz*. In case your plans change, you can buy a ticket at the door. The drama teacher thinks I'm really talented!

My best friend, McKenzie, kept asking Mom where you are. Mom wouldn't tell her. She (Mom) said you should tell her (McKenzie). So please let me know where you're living so McKenzie will stop asking about it.

Also, in case you lost my cell phone number or something, it's 555-0475.

Love,
Violet

"I told you he'd email you," McKenzie said the next day at lunch.

"You were right." I handed her a chunk of my brownie across the table. "Too bad he can't see the play."

McKenzie shrugged. "Not his fault he'll be out of town. And it's not like the play is on Broadway."

"Yeah. I should have quit when you did."

"You should have," McKenzie agreed.

"Ally is so annoying."

"Really?" McKenzie leaned toward me.

I wanted to tell her about Ally's parents and her freak-out about memorizing lines and the mean things she'd said about my dad. But McKenzie could never, ever know I'd been to Ally's house.

"Does Goldstein still act like Ally's the best actor ever?" McKenzie asked.

"Yeah. Even though she's totally not. Her parents fawn all over her too." I bit my lip. "I mean, I bet they do."

"I bet she has a huge bedroom and a walk-in closet for all her clothes. And one of those beds with a pink ruffled canopy. Her parents probably call her icky nicknames like Princess and Sweetheart."

None of those things were true. But I nodded and said, "She's no sweetheart, that's for sure."

NICKNAMES WE CAME UP WITH FOR ALLY
1. Alleycat
2. Alleytrash
3. Allison No Fun
4. The Snob

Before rehearsal that day, I walked up to Ally in the auditorium and said, "My dad sent me a really great email." Because I was mature, I did not add, "Told you so."

Ally grinned. "That's awesome, Violet!"

I frowned. I hadn't expected that reaction. I'd figured she'd make a snide comment or shrug or ignore me. I'd been so mad at her all week, but *she* didn't seem mad at *me*. She never seemed mad at anyone, not even Diego, who called her Shorty.

Why would she be mad at Diego though? Ally was easily in the top 20 percent for height for seventh-grade girls at our school. She was probably even in the top 13 percent. It wasn't like last year when Isabelle Noonan had called me mouse, which hurt because I was probably in the top 20 percent for mousiness. (Although McKenzie had cheered me up by calling Isabelle a rat, and saying mice are cute and run really fast and get to eat cheese all day.)

"I thought you'd look happier about hearing from your dad," Ally said. "I bet he's excited to see you in the play."

I felt my eyes narrow and my bottom lip curl.

"Are you okay?" Ally asked.

"Fine." I walked away and sat three rows back, on the other side of the aisle.

But I couldn't avoid her for long. Soon we were onstage together, rehearsing the scene where Dorothy meets the Cowardly Lion, right before my big song.

I had my part memorized, but Ally kept asking Mr. Goldstein for cues. The third time she did it, I mumbled, "Not again."

Mr. Goldstein gave me a sharp look.

Ally's lower lip trembled.

A few seconds later, she had to ask Mr. Goldstein for her line again.

"Shame on you," he said.

"Shame on you," Ally said.

"No," I said, which was not my line. "Shame on *you*, Ally, for not having your part memorized."

She made a little choking noise.

"That's enough, Violet." Mr. Goldstein's voice was as sharp as his glare.

Diego said, "For someone playing a lion with no nerve, you sure have a lot of nerve." He said it jokingly, but no one laughed. No one even smiled.

Then Kimmi Ito/the Wicked Witch said, "Violet, you should mind your own business."

"It *is* my business," I said. "Now I'll have to tell my dad not to come to the play, because the lead actor doesn't even know her lines."

"Stop, Violet. Not another word," Mr. Goldstein said.

Ally ran off the stage, through the auditorium, and outside. Kimmi followed her.

A few seconds later, the other girls followed them.

Not me. I stayed onstage and folded my arms over my flat

132

chest, trying to act tough. I probably just looked like I was hugging myself, which I was.

I wanted to run after the girls—run to Ally. I'd tell her I was sorry, tell her I knew she was trying hard, tell her it wasn't fair to expect her to learn her lines at the same time as me when she had a quadrillion more to memorize, tell her maybe she was right about my father. Even if he couldn't come to my play, couldn't he pick me up from school some time?

But I didn't do any of those things. I was as cowardly as the part I played.

My head pounded and my stomach gurgled, and I didn't know why I felt so bad. Was it for hurting Ally? Or for everyone at rehearsal hearing me hurt one of the most popular girls at school? Either way, I was a jerk.

Dad:

The play is going terrible. The girl who plays Dorothy doesn't know her lines. I got in a fight with her because of you. I was defending your honor. Are you honorable? It doesn't seem very honorable to go out of town the week of your daughter's play.

133

I tell you more in one email than I tell Mom in a week. But you don't tell me much at all—like even where you are.

Where are you?

Violet

FIFTEEN

$\mathcal{A}$lly knew most of her lines during Monday's rehearsal. Supposedly, the girls in the play—except me—had been getting together and helping her. After every line Ally got right, the girls—except me—clapped quietly or gave her a thumbs up.

Even Diego whispered, "You got this, Shorty," and Ally whispered back, "Thanks, Chubs," which weren't insults because Ally wasn't short and Diego wasn't chubby. They were more like nicknames between good friends. Or boyfriend and girlfriend.

No one cheered for me during rehearsal. They were probably booing me in their heads and thinking up new nicknames: Maleficent or Cruella de Vil or Lord Voldemort.

Mr. Goldstein kept picking on me. He said, "Positivity, Violet," and "You're in the glorious land of Oz. Bask in it," and "You're the Cowardly Lion, not the Surly Lion." Ally gave me a pitying look after he called me surly, which made me even surlier.

I stopped in the middle of pretending to hand Ally a bucket of water to throw over the witch. "Mr. Goldstein, acting would be a lot easier if we had props and costumes."

"Acting comes from within," Mr. Goldstein said. "*Feel* the props. *Feel* the costumes."

I kicked the imaginary bucket onto his annoying head and *felt* a little better.

Text to McKenzie: I hate actors. Mostly those named Ally.

McKenzie: ☹

Violet: Wanna do something Saturday night?

McKenzie: Sure

When rehearsal finally ended, Mr. Goldstein said, "Violet, I need to speak to you about your costume." He pointed to my phone. "I've noticed you're quite proficient at texting. Please text whomever is picking you up and inform them you'll be a few minutes late."

Text to Mom: Be out soon. Costume issue.

Ally gave me another pitying glance before walking out. Then it was just Mr. Goldstein and me, sitting with an empty seat between us about 30 percent of the way back in the auditorium, and a few kids gluing poppies onto a backdrop onstage.

"I was heavily involved in the theater throughout my schooldays," Mr. Goldstein said. "In high school, we did *Othello* and *Romeo and Juliet*. William Shakespeare knew how to write meaty parts!" He sounded infinitely more excited about Shakespeare than I was. That wasn't hard to do, given my subzero level of interest.

"Mr. Goldstein. Is there a problem with the Lion costume?" I asked.

"Pardon?" He tilted his head. "Oh. Our discussion has nothing to do with your costume. I was attempting to save you from embarrassment in front of the cast."

My heart sank. He was going to tell me again to show positivity. But how could I when Ally and the rest of the cast hated me, I'd betrayed my best friend by going to her enemy's house, and my dad was missing? My mom kept reminding me their separation wasn't my fault, which made it sound as if it *was* my fault. I mean, she didn't remind me that earthquakes and global warming weren't my fault, because those things definitely weren't.

"When I was growing up," Mr. Goldstein said, "boys weren't supposed to reveal their emotions. We could never show fear. And if a boy cried at school, he was done for."

"It's still like that," I said. "For girls too. You can't cry at school."

"It's a shame. So many kids are experiencing difficulties, but you'd never know it from looking at them."

Mr. Goldstein didn't know about my difficulties, did he?

He leaned forward. "The beautiful thing about acting is that one is *supposed* to reveal the character's emotions. In order to do so, one needs to explore one's own emotions."

I nodded. Mr. Goldstein was always telling us to dig deep.

"Rehearsals need to be a safe place for actors. Safe for you and safe for everyone in our little theater family." He stared at me hard.

"Safe for Ally," I said softly.

"Right."

"I didn't make things safe for her." My voice had turned whisper-soft. "I wrecked the rehearsal safe place."

Mr. Goldstein shook his head. "It's not wrecked. Merely a bit battered."

"I'm sorry." I blinked back tears. There was no crying at school.

"I know you're sorry, Violet. Why don't you let Ally know that too?"

Why? Because apologizing to a teacher for upsetting rehearsals was a lot easier than apologizing to a friend for upsetting her feelings. (Potential friend? Former friend?) Because for some strange reason, the worse your behavior was and the more you needed to apologize to someone, the harder it became. Because, really, I was a wimp.

$$\text{Amount of Harm} \times \text{Wimpiness of Wrongdoer} = \text{Difficulty of Apology}$$

"I am highly confident you can do better," Mr. Goldstein said.

I bit my lip. I wasn't highly confident. I wasn't even mediumly confident.

"Positivity, Violet. We'll build one another back up. That's what families do."

"Not all families." My voice came out as a whisper.

"Theater families build one another up," Mr. Goldstein said. "That's another beautiful thing about acting."

I gave him a small smile.

"If you're ready to go, I'll walk you out."

I nodded.

Before we left, Mr. Goldstein headed toward the stage and told the crew, "Those poppies look lovely."

"Great job," I said.

$$\pi$$

Grandpa Falls-Apart sputtered a few times before Mom got him started and drove out of the parking lot. "Did you solve the costume issue?" she asked.

"Uh-huh." My voice sounded small.

At the stop sign she usually rolled through, Mom came to a complete stop and stared at me. "Were there other issues too?"

"No," I murmured. I leaned against the car window and closed my eyes to get some peace. My brain kept picturing everyone cheering on Ally and giving me mean looks.

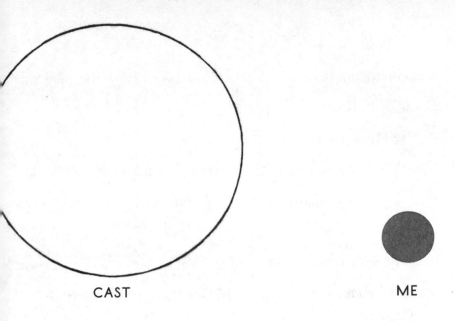

CAST

ME

The ride home seemed to take forever. I opened my eyes. We weren't on our way home. "Where are we?"

"Heading for Bonzo's Barbeque," Mom said.

"We are?"

Mom shrugged. "I know you like it. And we haven't been there in a long time."

"That's because you complained about it every time Dad wanted to go."

"Not every time," Mom said.

I thought about it and did the math. It was more like 60 percent of the time. "Okay. Well, thank you."

"You're welcome."

After we ordered our food, Mom asked how the play was going.

"Fine," I said.

"You seemed upset when I picked you up from rehearsal."

I put my napkin on my lap and stared at it. "Everything's fine."

"I wish you would talk to me more," Mom said. Her voice sounded sad—*yearning*, as Mr. Goldstein would say.

Telling Mom I'd been mean to Ally would make her even sadder. I took out my phone.

"Remember our rule," Mom said. "No phones at dinner."

"It's not *our* rule. It's *your* rule. Dad never cared."

"Put away your phone," Mom said gruffly.

I did. Then I looked around the restaurant. Two tables over, a couple laughed and chatted away like they were best friends, while their toddler sat in a booster seat with an iPad. I wished they were my parents.

Last Thanksgiving, my little cousin Liam had fallen asleep in his booster seat at the table. When my Aunt Amber started unbuckling him so she could carry him into the guest room, he'd woken up and said, "Where's my pie?"

Everyone around the table had laughed. Grandma had said, "He's got that Summers pie-loving gene," and everyone laughed again. Thanksgiving with Dad's relatives meant lots of laughing.

That's what I yearned for now—a family. I'd fractured our middle school theater family, and you could hardly call the forced duo of Mom and me a family. I wanted a real family with Mom and Dad and me, like I used to have.

The server brought our food: Boss of All Biscuits, Slab o' Ribs, Bacon & Bean Heaven, and Cream de la Cream Coleslaw for me. Plus peach pie for dessert. Mom got a boring salad.

I pushed away the bottle of Bonzo's World-Famous, Top-Secret Sauce, grabbed the bottle of ketchup, and slathered it on my ribs and beans. "You know, Mom," I said. "If you had gone here with Dad instead of complaining about this place, or—"

"Or!" Mom cut me off in a voice as sharp and steely as my steak knife. "Maybe if your dad had—" Then she cut *herself* off. She let out a big breath and said, "Just stop, Violet." The breath hadn't been big enough to let out the anger in her voice.

"No, no, no!" the boy in the booster seat shouted as his mother tried to take the iPad from him.

The dad grabbed the iPad, unbuckled the booster seat, picked up the little boy, and held him tight until he quieted down. The dad said, "I never get any peace."

"Baloney!" the mom said. "You hide out in your office all day."

"Mom," I said as I cut my ribs, gripping the knife like the boy had gripped the iPad. "You just told me you wished I'd talk to you. I did, and now you're all upset."

"Sometimes it's easier to write down your feelings." Mom's voice had returned to pity mode. "Would you like to email me?"

"What? That's totally dumb." It came out: "Wuh? Thaz towy duh," because my mouth was full.

"Fine!" Mom was no longer in pitying mode. She seemed mad. If Mom wrote down *her* feelings tonight, they would be 85 percent angry and 15 percent pity.

Mom could join the club of people who were mad at me: Ally; everyone else in the play; Dad, probably, after the last email I'd sent him. I was a horrible person.

"Do you know what my favorite food is?" Mom asked.

I shrugged.

"Sushi."

I made a face. "Raw fish. Gross."

Mom sighed. "That's what your father said whenever I brought it up. He would never go out for sushi with me."

I usually liked being compared to my dad, but not when it meant both of us acted mean to Mom. Had I gotten my horribleness from him? He was the one who'd disappeared. Mom was the one who'd taken me to Bonzo's.

"I bet you'd like sushi once you tried it," Mom said.

I would bet a lifetime of allowance money that I would not.

"Do you want to go to a sushi restaurant some time?" Mom asked hopefully.

"Sounds good," I lied.

Apparently, I wasn't a completely horrible person after all.

π

Early the next morning, I woke to sounds I hadn't heard in months. They were muffled, but I recognized them.

I turned on my phone. 2:48 a.m. Then I clicked on its flashlight, got out of bed, and slinked to the hallway. I stood there, frozen, listening to Mom's rhythmic sobs. I felt grateful, in a guilty way, that Mom's bedroom door was closed.

The steady sobs didn't let up. Mom did everything steadily, even crying. That's how I knew she would stop crying eventually. And as soon as her alarm went off, she'd get out of bed, splash water on her face, brew herself a big mug of coffee, remind me to get ready for school, and drive me there like everything was A-OK.

But she'd stop crying sooner if I called out to her or knocked on her door.

I didn't. I didn't make a sound. I didn't want to mother my mother. I'd never needed to. Mom was the steady one. Thankfully.

I skulked to my room and shut my door.

Then I turned on the light, took out some paper, and sat at my desk.

Dear Ally,

I'm very sorry I was so mean to you about not knowing your lines. I used to think you were stuck-up, but you're not. I acted like the stuck-up one. I was nervous about my dad.

Very sincerely,
Violet

Dear Ally,
I'm very sorry I was so mean to you about not knowing
your lines. I used to think you were stuck-up, but you're
not. I acted like the stuck-up one. ~~I was nervous about~~
~~my dad.~~

~~Very s~~Sincerely,
Violet

~~Dear~~ Ally,
I'm very sorry I was ~~so~~ mean to you about not knowing
your lines. ~~I used to think you were stuck-up, but you're~~
~~not. I acted like the stuck-up one.~~

Sincerely,
Violet

Ally,

I'm sorry ~~I was mean to you about not knowing your lines.~~

Violet

I ripped up my dumb tries at notes and threw the tiny pieces in the trash.

Then I grabbed my phone.

Text to Ally: I'm sorry.

SIXTEEN

HOW I SPENT MY MORNING

USUAL Things

I checked my email as soon as I woke up. Nothing from Dad.

When I rushed into the kitchen for my toast and peanut butter breakfast, Mom was sitting at the kitchen table, dressed and dry-eyed and clutching a large mug of coffee.

As I got out of the car, Mom told me to have a nice day.

RARE Things

I got ready for school quickly without Mom nagging me once.

We left for school almost fifteen minutes early.

I thanked Mom for driving me.

As soon as I got to school, I went right to Ally's locker. Actually, I stood about five feet away at a forty-five-degree angle so I wouldn't seem like a weird stalker, even though I was.

When Ally came by, I said, "Oh, hey," in a fake cheerleader voice unfortunately like my mom's.

"I got your text," Ally said like someone would say *I got dog poop on my shoe.*

"I'm sorry," I said, which was dumb, since I'd already texted her those two words (or three words if "I'm" counted as two words) and she'd just told me she got my text.

Ally wrinkled her nose as if she could smell the dog poop. "You texted me at, like, three in the morning."

I sighed. I couldn't even apologize right. "Oh, right. I hope the text didn't wake you up."

She walked right by me and faced her locker. "I didn't see it till I was eating breakfast."

"Phew! Because, you know, I've already apologized two times—the text and just now."

Ally didn't say anything, maybe because she was concentrating on twisting her combo lock. Not concentrating hard enough though, because her locker didn't open.

She spun the lock around and tried again. This time, the locker opened.

I moved closer to her and said, "But I would have apologized a third time if I *had* woken you up."

She took out *Treasure Island* and dropped it into her backpack. The *thud* sound stuck out in her silence.

"Because waking you up would have been a different thing to apologize for."

She dug through her backpack and put some notebooks in her locker.

"A whole separate apology," I went on.

I wasn't used to the silent treatment. McKenzie was never silent. Neither were my parents. Well, Dad had *gone* silent.

Ally closed her locker, spun the lock, and walked away without saying a word.

I sort of understood why my silences drove my mom up the wall.

If I had pen and paper handy and fifteen minutes to focus, I would have made a flowchart of my options:

One. Shout that Ally was the jerk for not accepting two apologies plus an offer for a third.

Two. Give the third apology.

Three. Think of something else to do.

But I didn't have pen and paper, or any time to focus. So I followed my instinct and ran down the hallway to catch up with Ally.

The Shin twins were walking toward us. They said, "Hey, Ally," at the same time. Nick Shin's voice had turned manly over the summer. Nate Shin's voice was still squeaky. Even though I had classes with both of them, neither of them acknowledged me.

As Ally waved to them, I told her, "I texted you in the middle of the night because I couldn't sleep."

Ally didn't stop walking or slow down or even look at me. But she said, "Why couldn't you sleep?"

I was so grateful for those four words. (Or five if you counted "couldn't" as two words.) They weren't as good as "Let's be friends again" or "I accept your apology" or "You're a nice person," but they were a lot better than silence.

"I couldn't sleep because I felt bad about being a jerk at rehearsal," I said. "I'm such a total idiot."

Ally slowed down. "You're not a total idiot."

"I'm at least a partial idiot. And a total jerk."

"Partial jerk," she said. She stopped walking.

"I'm really, really sorry." I was begging, but Ally deserved it, after how I'd treated her.

She looked at me, right into my eyes, and said, "Okay, I forgive you."

"Are you just saying that so I'll shut up?"

"Definitely." She laughed. "No, really I forgive you. Do you want to see a movie Saturday night? I'm going with some of the girls from the play."

I pictured myself huddling in the snack bar line with Ally and Sarah and Kimmi. The other girls would forgive me after seeing that Ally had. I could tell my joke about popcorn being healthy because corn is a vegetable, which McKenzie always laughed at.

Then I remembered I had plans with McKenzie. "Thanks a lot," I told Ally. "But I have someone coming over Saturday."

"Does she want to come to the movies too?"

I shook my head. "She doesn't like movies." Total lie. "But, yeah. Thanks. Sorry." I switched to a silly, sing-song voice. "Sorry. Sorry. Sorry."

We both laughed.

Something made me look down the hallway. McKenzie was walking toward us.

I quit laughing.

She glared at Ally, then turned and walked away.

"Is that who's coming over Saturday night?" Ally asked.

I stared at McKenzie's stiff back and her too-short jeans and nodded.

"I know she doesn't like me," Ally said.

"She likes you," I said. Another total lie. I kept staring down the hallway, even though McKenzie was gone. "Time for class."

We walked to Ally's classroom. "Let me know if you change your mind about the movie," she said before going inside.

I stood at the door for a moment, thinking that a month ago it would have seemed ridiculous for Ally and me to become friends. Now we weren't just becoming friends. We *were* friends.

I headed for my class and tried to figure out an explanation for McKenzie. I hoped I wouldn't see her before lunch.

Of course, she was waiting for me in front of my classroom. She said with a scowl, "For someone who texted me yesterday that you hated Ally, you sure seem to like her."

"Ally didn't do anything wrong," I said. "I was taking out my problems on her. I still don't know where my dad is, and I heard my mom crying, and—"

"So, you and Alleycat are BFFs now or something?"

"*You're* my BFF," I said.

McKenzie lost her scowl. She nodded. Maybe things would blow over.

They *could* have blown over—if McKenzie hadn't interrupted me when I was talking about my parents, or if I hadn't let the interruption bother me. But those things happened.

"You know what?" I said. "Ally's nice once you get to know her."

"I don't want to get to know her. I barely get to see you anymore, with all your rehearsals."

"Yeah. I'm glad we're getting together Saturday night." Not a total lie, but sort of one.

"Let's go to the movies," McKenzie said.

I pictured us running into Ally and the other girls at the theater. Ally would ask us to sit with her, and McKenzie would scowl again, and I wouldn't know what to do. So I said, "Can you just come over?"

"You're always telling me what to do these days," McKenzie said.

"Sorry."

If Ally had heard me apologize, she probably would have

told me to stop. But McKenzie didn't. She kept talking. "Ask your mom to pick me up, okay?" She didn't wait for my okay back. "She'll be so thrilled to hurl questions at us."

I felt my face tighten. It was different for me to complain about my mom than for McKenzie to do it. Or anyone, really. I didn't like it when Dad did it either.

"My mom's not a Free-Range Kids mom," I said. "But she's not bad."

McKenzie nodded. "Yeah. Your mom is kind of great."

Text from Ally: Seeing *Love Sucks* at Valley Theater tomorrow at 730. R u sure u can't come

Violet: Sorry AGAIN. ☺ Can't. ☹

SEVENTEEN

A lot of weird things happened with McKenzie on Saturday. Mom picked her up from her house—really from the sidewalk in front of her house. That wasn't weird. McKenzie came over for sleepovers a lot, and that was the usual arrangement. Judging from the last time Mom tried to go into McKenzie's house, Mom wasn't welcome there.

But after McKenzie got in the back seat with me and we pulled away from the curb, Mom said she'd been shopping at the mall yesterday. Weird Thing Number One.

"Huh?" I said, because I knew Mom hated shopping. She wasn't like the *Real Housewives of Orange County* on TV, who spent approximately 25 percent of their waking hours shopping, 25 percent getting beauty/surgical treatments, 25 percent drinking, and 25 percent feuding with one another. Mom barely did any *Real Housewives of Orange County* things, except for feuding when Dad lived with us. She did not shop at the mall.

Mom said, "I stumbled onto a fantastic sale and saw some clothes that shouted your name."

"I didn't know clothes could shout," I joked.

McKenzie smiled at me and Mom laughed, but it sounded like a fake laugh. She said, "So I bought them. You know I can't resist a bargain."

The can't-resist-a-bargain part was true. Last year, Mom had filled one of our kitchen cupboards with cans of pea soup on sale for ten cents apiece. I used to like pea soup.

"You bought me bargain clothes?" I grumbled.

"Just because they were on sale doesn't mean they're not nice. They're in the bag on the back seat," Mom said. "And the clothes are for McKenzie, not you." Weird Thing Number Two.

McKenzie reached into the paper tote bag between us and pulled out a navy-blue sweater, a red long-sleeved T-shirt, a white cotton nightgown, and two pairs of jeans. Then she quickly stuffed them back in the bag and said, "Thank you."

"Mom, you always say you hate shopping," I said.

Mom didn't respond.

"And how do a solid-colored sweater and T-shirt and cotton nightgown and Levi's shout McKenzie's name?" Weird Thing Number Three.

"Because they . . ." Mom trailed off.

"You know red is my favorite color," McKenzie said, which only explained the red T-shirt.

"You didn't find anything that shouted Violet?" I asked Mom.

She glanced at me. "The last time I bought clothes for you, you said you wanted to pick out your own things because you didn't want to dress like a middle-aged mother."

She had a point. Mackenzie could use some new clothes, but it still felt kind of weird.

"Mom," I said, "I don't get why you were out browsing and why—"

"See that gray house?" she interrupted me.

"I see it," McKenzie said.

"Can you believe there was a bidding war for that?" Mom asked excitedly, like the house had a UFO on its lawn instead of a SOLD sign. "The seller got an all-cash deal twenty thousand dollars over the asking price."

"Well, it *is* on a corner lot," McKenzie said, as if she cared about real estate.

"True," Mom said.

"And it's only a few blocks from the elementary school."

"You have quite the eye for real estate, McKenzie," Mom said.

I groaned, but McKenzie smiled and said, "Thanks, Ms. Summers." Weird Thing Number Four.

Dinner wasn't weird—mac and cheese and soggy green beans. Mom offered to heat up some pea soup, but even McKenzie was tired of it. As usual, Mom asked about our teachers and what we were learning and homework assignments, but we vagued out on her. I hadn't told Mom about my advanced math assignments. She knew I was good at math, but I didn't think she knew I had a "remarkable flair for mathematics," as Ms. Merriweather had written on my last supplemental assignment. If Mom ever found out, she'd expect me to get *A*s in math for the rest of my life.

After dinner, McKenzie said, "You know what's fun?

Hate-watching the Kardashians. I bet one of their shows is on now. They're always on. Let's check."

McKenzie was right about the show being on, but wrong about it being fun to hate-watch. It was boring. And as soon as I made my first hate-watch comment, McKenzie said Kris Jenner looked really good for her age and was a great mother to six kids.

Then I realized McKenzie wasn't hate-watching the show. She was love-watching it. Weird Thing Number Five.

My brain wandered. I wondered if the *Love Sucks* movie was any good. Even if it wasn't, if I were seeing it with Ally and the other girls tonight, I probably could have joked about it and they wouldn't have gotten upset.

I looked at McKenzie, who was staring at the TV. I got an idea about tonight's Weird Things. First, I noticed McKenzie's sweater was tight on her and the sleeves were too short. Then I saw her jeans were frayed on the bottom—and not on-purpose, stylish frayed. Finally, I understood why Mom made up that story about finding a bargain with McKenzie's name on it while shopping at the mall. None of it seemed weird anymore—more like nice.

HOW MOM SPENDS HER TIME

Talking about real estate

Nagging

Working in real estate

Asking me questions

Doing nice things

Eating

"You know what?" I said. "Those clothes my mom found do look like your style."

McKenzie kept staring at the TV, but she nodded.

EIGHTEEN

*A*s soon as McKenzie left Sunday morning, I hurried to my bedroom and checked my email.

Yes! Dad! I *knew* he'd email me back.

Dear Violet,

I'm sorry I haven't seen you since I left. I'm working some things out in my life. I love you very much.

Your mother and I think it would be good for you to see a therapist to help you sort out issues about our separation. It would be better to talk about your issues face-to-face with your mother and/or a therapist than through emails with me.

Love,
Dad

My eyes narrowed, blurring Dad's words on my laptop. I wanted to punch it and throw it against the wall. I let out a long, strange noise, a growl/roar that sounded something like, "Awkgrrawhuh!"

Mom knocked on my door. "Are you all right, Violet?"

I ran to my door, threw it open, and shouted, "You talked to Dad and didn't even tell me? Why didn't I get to talk to him too? And you both think I shouldn't email him and I need a therapist?"

"Oh, Violet." Mom's face crumpled like she was going to cry. As if she had any right to. "I wish your dad would talk to you. I can't force—"

I slammed the door shut. I was angry and had every right to be—stuck with a mom who was in my face all the time, and a dad who was never in my face and never in my house and never, ever anywhere near me. Where in the world was he anyway? What was he hiding?

I got out my phone and called him, jabbing the screen hard, as if that would show him how angry I was.

I didn't know what I was going to say to him, but I didn't care. I just needed to talk to him. I needed *him* to talk to *me*.

He didn't answer.

The only message I left was, "Da-a-a-ad," which sounded whiny, not angry. Embarrassing.

I hung up and clenched the phone tight in my hand.

Then I plopped on my bed and scrolled through my contact list. McKenzie knew all about my family. She'd understand.

But I didn't call her. Because she'd probably start talking about herself again and I absolutely could not take that.

I stared at the screen. Ally? She wouldn't understand, not with her nice parents and cute sisters and perfect life.

Then I called Dad again and left a calmer message: "Dad, I don't need therapy. I just need to talk to you. Call me and tell me what's going on."

I sat on my bed and waited for him to call me back.

But he didn't.

So I left another message. And another. And another. They all said the exact same two words: "Call me."

I filled up his voicemail box. Now he'd have to listen to me: "Call me. Call me! CALL ME! CALL ME! CALL ME! CALL ME! CALL ME! CALL ME!"

NINETEEN

I checked my phone as soon as I woke the next morning.

Nothing.

And as soon as I got out of the shower.

Nothing.

And on the way to school while my mom talked about the tennis court or volleyball court or basketball court or whatever was on the lot of her supposedly magnificent real estate listing.

Nothing, except McKenzie butt-dialed me and I heard nineties music and a raspy cough, which meant her mom was driving her to school for a change.

I only checked my phone once in math class, because I wanted Ms. Merriweather to keep trusting me to work on my own. If I had to pretend to pay attention in class while she explained the differences between a circle and a sphere and between a sphere and a spear, I'd find a spear to stab through my ears.

I checked my phone every time I got bored in history class. Ms. Killjoy (real name: Ms. Kilroy) was going on about the amazing steam engine, so I checked my phone about a quadrillion times.

A quadrillion more nothings.

"Violet, do you want your phone taken away?" Killjoy asked.

"Sorry," I mumbled. I looked at the time on my phone. Class wouldn't be over for another twenty minutes. I couldn't imagine waiting that long without checking my phone again. So I said, "My great-grandmother is dying. I need to check for news."

"I thought your great-grandmother died last month, when your Revolutionary War essay was due."

"That was my other great-grandmother."

Killjoy raised her eyebrows.

Keely Washington cracked, "Girl, you're running out of relatives," and most of the class laughed.

Actually, both my great-grandmothers were ridiculously healthy. My Nana Susan headed a Friends of the Library program, and my Nana Judy played tennis twice a week. But I really was checking for news—from my dad—so I hadn't lied that much.

Dad didn't call during class or while I walked to the cafeteria. So I gazed at my phone at lunchtime as McKenzie and I sat across from each other in our usual corner, just us and an overwhelming stink of overcooked broccoli and disgusting beef stew and annoying fits of laughter from kids whose parents never told them to stop emailing them.

McKenzie was talking about the road trip her family went on before her dad died. "Best vacation of my life," she said. Apart from our disappointing Girl Scout camping trip, it was the *only* vacation of her life I'd heard about—and I'd heard about it at least twice before. She said, "My first time in the mountains and my first time seeing bear cubs."

"Last time you told that story, you said it was dark outside and they may have been raccoons," I said.

"You're so pissy today," McKenzie said.

I was. A true best friend would have apologized. A true best friend would have pretended not to have heard McKenzie's story before.

But . . . a true best friend would get to talk too. Mr.

Goldstein said every character was the star of their own story. I was done being the quiet sidekick in McKenzie's story.

I said, "I'm in a pissy mood because I left a ton of messages on my dad's voicemail and he hasn't called back."

"At least you *have* a dad to leave messages for," McKenzie said.

"At least *your* dad didn't leave you voluntarily," I said.

McKenzie glared at me. "I can't believe you, Violet."

I could hardly believe me either. I'd been rude and maybe even mean to my best friend. And instead of trying to back down, I said, "I can't believe *you*, McKenzie. You're always making things about yourself."

Then we got quiet for a long time, which wasn't like us. At least it wasn't like McKenzie, who was probably dying to say something. She never stayed quiet. Even when you were supposed to, like at the movies and in class, she still whispered stuff. But now, with both of us so mad, talking would mean surrendering. We even ate our sandwiches quietly. Mine, tuna on wheat. McKenzie's, ham on white—probably. I refused to look at her to make sure. I knew I could out-silence a silence-hater like McKenzie.

I thought about her dumb contest about who had it worse

in the dad department. How did you even win that contest? By having it the worst or the best? Not that either of us had it the best. Someone like Ally had it the best. Or the daughter of a billionaire, as long as he wasn't one of those evil billionaire bad guys in movies. If I were a billionaire, I wouldn't spend my time plotting to destroy the world. I'd hang out in my gigantic swimming pool with water slide and Jacuzzi, and have my personal assistant bring me baked goods.

I looked at my phone again. Nothing from Dad. He was far from a billionaire, but he could still hang out with me and maybe take me to a bakery.

My thoughts churned back to who had it worse in the dad department. It was complicated. I tried to list different dad situations in my head, but that got even more complicated. So I took my pen and notebook out of my backpack and started writing.

DAD SITUATIONS FROM BAD TO WORST

1. Your dad isn't home much because of work.

2. Your dad isn't home much because of fun (bars and gambling).

3. Your dad says he's working, but your mom accuses him of really being at a bar or casino.

I stared at my notebook. All three of those situations were about the same dad: mine.

"What are you writing?" McKenzie asked.

I *knew* I could out-silence her.

I didn't answer. I didn't even look up. I wasn't trying to be mean. I was just concentrating on the list. But I didn't *mind* being mean.

I heard McKenzie playing a game on her phone. I pulled my notebook closer to my side of the table, put my hand over what I'd written, and continued my list.

DAD SITUATIONS FROM BAD TO WORST

4. Your dad moves out because of your mom. He still sees you.

5. Your dad moves out because of your mom. He doesn't see you.

6. Your dad moves out because of you. He doesn't see you.

7. Your dad dies.

8. Your dad moves out because of you. And he doesn't see you. And then he dies.

I probably qualified for number five. So McKenzie, at number seven, had it worse than me. Death is the most extreme worst thing.

But even though my dad was alive, I should have been able to complain about him without McKenzie saying, "At least you have a dad."

When the bell rang, I still didn't talk to McKenzie or even make eye contact with her. I put my notebook in my backpack and gathered my lunch trash to throw out.

I was about to stand up when McKenzie kicked my shin, hard, under the table.

"Ow!" I glared at her.

"Oops." She shrugged.

"That was really, really mean!" I said.

By the time I thought about kicking her back, she'd already stood and started walking away, her head held high as if she couldn't care less about what had just happened.

In a horrible way, I was glad she'd kicked me. Now I had a solid reason to quit our friendship.

TWENTY

$\mathcal{W}$hen my phone finally rang that day, it was after school and I was rehearsing onstage. I was barely listening to Ally's beautiful singing, even though Mr. Goldstein always said listening techniques separated the pro actors from the amateurs. He also said to silence your cellphones at rehearsals. I hadn't listened to that either. I was definitely an amateur.

I grabbed my phone from my back pocket, looked at the caller ID, and let out a long breath of worried air I'd been storing since last night.

Then I hurried downstage and jumped off. "Dad," I said as soon as I landed.

"Violet," Mr. Goldstein said testily in front of me.

"Violet," Dad said testily in my ear.

I walked away from Mr. Goldstein, who repeated my name more testily.

"Her grandmother's dying in the hospital," Kimmi said.

"*Great*-grandmother," Diego said.

"You two have poor listening techniques," Sarah said. "It's Violet's great-aunt."

I hurried to the side exit.

"Violet?" Ally called out. She was the first person to say my name without sounding testy. She sounded concerned.

I walked out of the auditorium and closed the door behind me. I didn't know how this phone call would go, but at least I knew I could talk to my father. McKenzie could never talk to hers again. I shouldn't have been so mean to her.

"What's going on, Vi?" Dad asked. His voice was softer now, and I wondered if he missed me as much as I missed him, or at least almost as much, because it would be hard to match how much I missed him. He said, "You and your mother left so many messages, you filled up my voicemail."

"Mom called you?" Each word came out like a panicky gasp.

"Violet, what's wrong?" Dad's voice seemed testy again. Mom used to say he had no patience. Dad used to say he just didn't suffer fools.

I didn't want to be a fool who made him suffer, so

I said, "Everything's wrong. But I don't need a therapist."

"What?"

"I said I don't need a therapist." I kept walking away from the auditorium.

"Okay. It would be hard to come up with the money for that anyway," Dad said.

It should have made me relieved that I'd won that fight. But it hadn't been a fight. I wished he'd put up some kind of fight, or at least a small protest, to show he cared.

I hadn't filled up his voicemail and checked my phone a quadrillion times and walked out of rehearsal for nothing. So I said, "I don't understand why you can't see me."

He didn't respond. It was like today's mostly silent lunch with McKenzie. If I had been sitting across from Dad, I might have kicked his shin, like McKenzie. Or possibly tried to hug him.

But I wasn't sitting across from him. I was miles away from him—maybe fifty miles, maybe a thousand, I didn't even know. I wasn't sitting either. I was standing by myself on gray asphalt, between the side of the auditorium and a dumpster. It was cold outside—a near record low for Orange County this time of year, the TV weather lady had gushed excitedly—and my jacket was inside.

I couldn't play the silent game with Dad like I had with McKenzie. It was a terrible game. Plus, I didn't know how long I could keep Dad on the phone. What if he hung up on me? So I said, "When are you coming back, anyway?"

"Violet, I'm not moving back with you and your mother." He used that firm/weary/pitying tone my mother used. It sounded even worse from him, because he'd hardly ever been firm, weary, or pitying with me before.

"I wasn't asking you to move back in with us," I said. Though I did want him to move back, so he and Mom could solve their problems and we could stay a family. "I meant when are you coming back to town?"

"What?"

"Where are you? You said in your email you'd be out of town so you can't see my play, which is coming up soon."

"What email, Violet?"

Why did he have to make everything so hard? "You wrote me those emails," I said. "You told me I need a therapist. You're the one who needs a therapist if you can't even remember what you wrote your daughter about or what city or state you're in."

"I don't understand," Dad said, sounding impatient.

I used to think he was the only one who understood me. But now he didn't even understand my simple questions about his emails or where he was. "Have you been drinking?" I asked, sounding horribly like my mom.

"No, Violet." He had the same annoyed tone he used with Mom. He had never sounded like that with me before, though I had never asked him if he'd been drinking. "Violet, listen to me. I didn't send you any emails. I'm not going out of town."

I stood with the phone clenched in my hand, trying to make sense of things. I crossed my arm over my chest to keep out the cold, but it was impossible.

Dad hated silence as much as McKenzie did. So he said, "Vi, I'm going to be straight with you."

"You weren't straight with me before?"

He ignored that and plunged in. "I'm taking a break from responsibility. You only have one life, right? I was spending most of my life working or looking for work or pretending to look for work to fend off your mother, and running errands or fixing things around the house or doing yardwork. Your mother loves the domestic stuff, the routine. She insisted on the three of us eating dinner at the table every night like one of those old-fashioned families. But that's never been my style."

"You didn't like eating dinner together?" I said softly.

"I did, Vi. But not with all those rules—same time every night, no cell phones at the table, no TV. And the arguing was too much. I need to simply be me for a while, without so many responsibilities, without being a husband or father or—"

"But you *are* a father. You're *my* father."

He didn't respond.

I stood with the hard, silent phone against my ear. This was the worst Dad Situation ever. It was number quadrillion on the list. I wished this were only a scene from a play, a tragic one where I was a fictional character shivering in the cold at a dreary school on a gray day near a smelly dumpster.

It would be the dumbest play in the world. No one would ever see it. No one would want my pitiful part.

I didn't want to play that part, to be that character. Not anymore. I cleared my throat and pretended to be the Lion—the "not actually cowardly" Lion charging at the Witch of the West. "How dare you send me emails telling me you—"

Dad interrupted me. "Whatever the emails were telling you, they didn't come from me."

I'd been about to say *telling me you loved me.*

He added, "I don't know what kind of jerk would send you fake emails in my name, but it wasn't me."

I closed my eyes so I could think. The dumpster stench filled my nose and Dad's words burned my ears. But I figured it out. I realized what kind of jerk would send me emails in Dad's name. A lying, interfering jerk.

"Listen, Vi," Dad said, unnecessarily because I'd *been* listening. I'd been listening so hard. I'd been hanging on to his every word—not only now, but all my life. He said, "Your mother wanted me to see a therapist."

Of course she did.

"Actually, she wanted both of us to go. Marital counseling, it's called. But that's not my style. I don't like strangers trying to figure me out or tell me what to do," Dad said, like that was something to be proud of. "But that's just me. I've always been a free spirit. What I'm getting at, Violet, is maybe you *should* see a therapist. You sounded really upset on the phone last night."

I kept my eyes closed and wished he weren't my dad. I wished he were only an actor playing a dad, a horribly selfish dad. I wished my real dad was like Ally's nice, annoying dad—or even McKenzie's saintly dead one.

And I wished again, I wished so hard that I were only an actor playing the part of Violet—pathetic Violet, shaking outside in the cold, too dumb to have taken her jacket, wanting something she couldn't have, someone who didn't really exist.

"The therapist will probably say I'm a bad father and blame all your problems on me," the dad character said. *"But I think our time apart will be a positive, not just for me, but for you and your mother, too."*

The actor playing Violet opened her eyes and barked out a laugh.

No, actually, *I* barked out a laugh. If this really were a scene from a play, it would be a comedy. No one could take my dad's dialogue seriously.

As he rambled on about his need for solitude and search for meaning, I moved close to the dumpster to give his words the stinky setting they deserved.

"Violet?" Ally called out. She and Diego stood outside the auditorium door. Ally was holding my jacket.

They started walking toward me, looking around.

I clicked off my phone as if it were nothing, ran behind the dumpster, and crouched there like a movie hero setting up a surprise attack on a bad guy.

But the only bad guy was my dad, and I'd hung up on him.

The dumpster smelled awful. I plugged my nose and stayed still. Luckily, Ally and Diego hadn't seen me. I just had to wait until they gave up looking for me.

"She ran somewhere behind this dumpster," Diego said. He must have walked closer, because he wasn't shouting, and I could hear him fine.

Great move, Violet. Nothing like wading in soggy trash behind a stinky dumpster so you can be seen by the boy you've had a crush on for the last fourteen months.

"I'll talk to her," Ally said. She was right near the dumpster too. "Go back to rehearsal, Diego. Tell Mr. Goldstein we're sorry for leaving, okay?"

"I can stay," Diego said, because he's a guy, and guys always want to stay with a beautiful girl like Ally, even if it means suffering with a pathetic girl in soggy trash behind a stinky dumpster.

"I got this," Ally said.

"Mr. Goldstein will want you back in rehearsal. You're the star of the play," Diego said.

"I'm also Violet's good friend."

That would have made me happy if I weren't so sad.

"I like Violet, too," Diego said.

Like liked me or just liked me? Either way, that would have made me happy too.

"Let me talk to her alone," Ally said.

I heard footsteps walking away from me. Then I heard other footsteps coming toward me.

"Violet, can we talk somewhere away from the dumpster?" Ally asked.

I didn't say anything.

The footsteps came close—right to the edge of the trash. Ally really *was* a good friend.

I walked to her, stopping halfway to shake off the slimy wet cardboard and weird plastic stuff from the bottom of my shoes.

Ally threw my jacket around my shoulders and gave me a hug.

Then I did something almost as embarrassing as hiding behind a dumpster. I burst into tears. Not pretty, soft ones, like Ally's that night at her house. More like loud, snotty, croaky, ugly crying. Also, I was shaking from the cold and/or the phone call and/or total humiliation.

It felt like I cried and shook for an hour, but it was probably only a few minutes. Then I stopped shaking and cried more normally for like a minute, and then I stopped crying but felt really sad. Ally kept hugging me the whole time.

After I stepped back, Ally said, "I'm sorry about your great-aunt."

I laughed. "She's dead."

Ally took a step back.

"Not my great-aunt. I mean, she *is* dead, but she died before I was born."

Ally frowned.

"It's really my dad," I explained.

"Your dad died?" Ally asked, scrunching her eyebrows.

I wish, I thought for a half second. (Or maybe two or three seconds.)

"I'm *so* sorry," Ally said.

I shook my head. "My dad's alive. He's fine, I guess. He just called to tell me to stop trying to talk to him. He told me he didn't want any responsibilities—me and my mom being the responsibilities."

"Oh, Violet," Ally said, as though this was even worse than if my dad had died. It wasn't, not according to my Dad Situations from Bad to Worst list. But it felt like the worst thing ever.

"Hey!" Diego shouted. He hurried toward us, panting as he ran. He was one of those people who may look like they're in good shape because they're thin, but really aren't. I was one of those people too. We had so much in common. We also both had straight brown hair.

Diego reached us quickly. He was breathing hard and his face was red and shiny, but he was still perfect. He panted, "Goldstein. Wants. You. Inside."

I nodded.

But Ally said, "We need a few minutes."

"Mr. Goldstein said ASAP." Diego was breathing better now.

Ally and I didn't move.

"As soon as possible," Diego said, like we didn't know what ASAP meant.

"It'll be possible *later,* not now," Ally said. "Give us a few minutes."

Diego didn't move, except to cross his arms.

"Thanks, Diego. Bye," Ally said.

"Well, hurry up." He slowly walked away, glancing back every so often.

"Thanks for staying out here with me, Ally," I said. "You won't tell anyone about my dad, will you?"

Ally shook her head.

"It's so embarrassing," I muttered to the ground.

Ally cleared her throat as if she was going to talk. But she didn't. There was only silence. Then she cleared her throat again and said very quietly, "I don't even know who my dad is."

"What?" I looked at her, but she was looking away. I said, "Your dad is nice. I met him at your house, remember?"

And then pretty, popular, perfect Ally told me a bunch of stuff.

STUFF ALLY TOLD ME

1. The people I had met at her house were her grandparents.

2. She'd lived with them since she was four, and on and off before that.

3. Her mom claimed she didn't know who Ally's dad was, but Ally wasn't sure whether to believe her. Ally's mom had told her a lot of lies, like:

    a. She was going to take Ally out for her birthday last year.

    b. She had given up drugs for good.

    c. She wanted Ally and her other daughters to live with her.

        i. But according to Ally, she wanted drugs more.

4. Ally was going to track down her dad one day, just to get child support to pay back her grandparents.

    a. I wondered if there were other reasons too.

    b. I didn't wonder that out loud.

5. Ally had found out she was 40 percent Mexican because of an online DNA test her grandparents let her do.

6. The little girls I had met were really Ally's half-sisters.

7. They knew who their dad was, but he was in jail, which was probably worse than not knowing who your dad was.

8. The last time Ally saw her mom, she was "strung out" and her grandparents had to call the police.

9. Sometimes she still thought her mom would get clean and take care of her and they'd live happily ever after.

10. But mostly she didn't think that anymore.

Ally was matter-of-fact when she said it. All of it.

But I wasn't matter-of-fact when I heard it. I said "Oh, Ally" at least three times. I couldn't think of much else to say. Ally's dad being a mystery was even worse than my dad taking his stupid responsibility break. I wasn't sure where "You don't know who your dad is" or Ally's half-sisters' "Your dad's in jail" fell on my list of Dad Situations from Bad to Worst, but they were awful.

Ally gave a little shrug and said, "So let's neither one of us be embarrassed about our fathers."

I couldn't help saying, "Oh, Ally," one more time.

Then Diego came outside again and shouted, "We really need you guys in rehearsal!"

"Are you ready?" Ally asked me.

I nodded. "Are *you* ready?"

Ally nodded.

She took my hand, which probably would have felt weird

any other time. We walked over to Diego, and back to the auditorium.

When we got inside, My Goldstein said, "Violet, I'm sorry about your . . ." He trailed off.

"Great-aunt," Ally said.

"Dad," I said at the same time.

Mr. Goldstein's eyebrows shot up.

"She means her dad called during rehearsal, even though he should have known what Violet was doing and not disturbed her," Ally said. "Violet's dad is the one who should be sorry. Very sorry. He's rude."

"Yeah." I nodded gratefully at Ally. "He's really rude."

"Violet, are you up to rehearsing with your theater family?" Mr. Goldstein asked.

I locked arms with Ally and Diego. "Let's follow the yellow brick road."

TWENTY-ONE

"*How* was rehearsal?" my mom asked when I got in the car.

I didn't even say my usual *fine*. I just stared out the window into the dark.

"I felt terrible last night, hearing how upset you were about your dad," Mom said as she pulled out of the parking lot. "Especially because it's partly my fault. I made a terrible decision."

For a second, I thought she was going to say something like *I never should have let your dad go.* But I knew what her terrible decision was. I'd figured it out on the phone today. It was a no-brainer, once I realized my dad wouldn't have sent those nice emails.

"I deceived you, Violet. I thought I was doing a good

thing at the time, but I wasn't. Then it snowballed." Her voice cracked like a sixth-grade boy's. "I have to stop it before it gets any more out of hand, even though you're going to be furious with me, as well you should."

I nodded. For the first time ever, Mom was telling me I should be furious with her. I had been furious with her many times before when she hadn't told me to be. Tonight I was mad at her, but not really furious.

"It may be hard for you to believe," Mom said in an even crackier voice. "But I love you more than anything."

It actually wasn't hard to believe, but I still kept staring out the window. Just because you love someone doesn't mean you can't do something wrong to them—something very, very wrong.

"I wanted to make things easier for you," she said.

"Ha," I muttered, not in a ha-ha laughing way.

"Like when you were little, and I'd kiss a scrape on your knee and tell you that would make it better."

"I'm not little," I said. I was done muttering. "And kisses don't make scrapes go away any faster. They could even infect the scrapes and make them worse."

"I have no excuse for what I did. It's awful."

I turned to her. "You pretended you were Dad and sent me emails."

She let out a little gasp. "You knew?"

"I figured it out today."

She pulled over and parked at a curb, even though we were only a few blocks from our house.

I stared at Mom's nervous face, at her hands gripping the steering wheel of the parked car. When I spoke, there wasn't much anger in my voice—about 15 percent anger and 70 percent sadness and 15 percent curiosity. "How did you even do that? Did you hack into Dad's email account?"

"I went into his account after you told me you'd emailed him. I felt bad for you, so I . . . I know I made things worse, but at the time I thought I was helping."

I shook my head. "Yeah, big help."

"I'm sorry," she said again.

"So you read Dad's personal emails," I pointed out.

"I read his junk email account, the one he gives out to salespeople so his real address doesn't fill up with spam."

"It's the one on all my school forms. His junk email is the only one I know about."

"Oh, Violet," Mom said, her tone now pitying.

I looked out my window again so she wouldn't see me blinking back tears. "How did you know Dad's password?"

"He's always used the same password: Violet. Number sign. One."

"As if I'm number one in his life. Ha," I said.

"I'm so sorry, Violet. It was stupid and wrong of me."

"Your apology is about as useful as a kiss on a knee." I glared at her, but it was too dark for my glare to hurt her. Anyway, she already seemed pretty hurt.

I pictured her kissing my knee after I fell off my bike the first day I rode it without training wheels. As I'd pedaled, Dad had held on to the back of the bike, steadying it and promising he wouldn't let go. But after a few minutes, he gave the bike a push and let go. I'd ridden down a small slope that seemed like the Alps, panicked, and fallen down.

Mom had yelled, "Why did you do that?"

"You nagged me to teach her to ride her bike," Dad had complained. "And when I do, you scream at me."

Mom had brought me inside, washed my knee, and kissed it. And her kiss did seem to make my knee feel better.

The next day, she'd driven me and my bike to a flat, grassy

park. Then she walked beside me for hours, holding on to the bike as I pedaled. She did it again the next day. Eventually, with my say-so, she'd let go and I'd learned to ride.

I cleared my throat and said, "I finally got Dad to talk to me today."

"Oh?" Her voice was fake calm.

"All I had to do was call him a quadrillion times and fill up his voicemail. He called back to tell me to leave him alone."

Mom mumbled something that sounded like a very bad word. Then she took a big breath and said, "That's his loss."

I nodded. I didn't feel mad at her anymore.

"Violet, what happened with me and him is not your—"

"Fault. I know. You keep telling me that."

"Because it's true," Mom said.

"I know," I said automatically. Except now I believed it. What happened was hardly Mom's fault either, I realized. It was mostly because of Dad. He stopped thinking of anyone else, or maybe he never did that much in the first place. If Dad was so sick of Mom's nagging, why didn't he just put away his shoes for once or go to the market when he promised he would?

And wasn't it better to have a parent nagging you about doing well in school than one who wouldn't even give your school his real email address? Maybe a lot of what Dad called "nagging" was actually Mom trying to help our family. I suddenly saw all this and wondered why I hadn't seen it before.

"I love you, Mom," I said.

"I love you, too." Mom leaned over and put her arms around me. "I promise not to lie to you anymore or keep secrets."

I sat up straight. "So tell me where Dad's been hiding out."

"Oh, Violet." Mom sighed. "He's renting an apartment at the Shoreham Arms."

But that was only a few miles from our house. It was where he'd taken me to sneak into the pool.

I let out a little whimper. I'd always thought math could solve my parents' problems and make us a true family, but it's impossible to bring two people together when one of them refuses to be part of the equation.

Mom wrapped her arms around me tighter and I pressed myself against her.

Will Summers
Shoreham Arms Apts.
242 Morgridge Way, #6
Cypress, CA 90630

Dear Dad,

Mom gave me your address. Don't worry. I won't be writing you, calling you, or emailing you again. And I'm not writing you to try to get you and Mom back together or remind you about my play. I just want to tell you that I might not be so eager to talk to you when you're ready to talk to me. A lot has happened with me, schoolwise and friendwise and me getting wise, or wiser at least—wise enough to know that what you're doing is very unwise.

Well, take care of yourself. Though no one needs to tell you that.

Sincerely,

Violet

TWENTY-TWO

*A*t lunch the next day, I stood by the entrance to the cafeteria. First, I looked at McKenzie. She was sitting by herself in our usual spot, her shoulders hunched, staring at her phone. Then I looked at Ally. She sat in the middle of the cafeteria with Zahara Khalil, who was even more beautiful than her beautiful name. Zahara modeled for a magazine ad and had been in a commercial for Orange County's Best Ice Cream. This year she'd started wearing a hijab, which showed off her perfect cheekbones and gorgeous dark eyes. I wondered if Zahara had gone on dates like Ally supposedly had.

If I were brave, I would have marched to their table and plopped myself between them. But I was not brave. I did not march or plop.

Except I wasn't Cowardly Violet anymore either. So I

slowly walked to their table, thinking about what to say when I got there. *Hi?* Or *Mind if I sit here?* Or maybe—

"Violet!" Ally gave me a small wave.

I waved back like I was stranded on an island and she was the first sign of life I'd seen in a week.

I dropped my stupid arms. But I kept walking over.

When I got near her, Ally said, "Hey, Violet. Do you know if that ancient bowling alley by City Hall is still open?"

Had she called me over only for that?

"Because Zahara and I were talking about going bowling. Do you like to bowl?"

I loved to bowl with my parents. Used to, anyway. Mom was all about the technique: Take three steps, bend your knee, shake hands with the ball. But Dad would just run over and hurl his ball. I was always Team Dad at the bowling alley. It was more fun to throw the ball down the lane fast and wild.

"Violet?" Ally said.

"I think that bowling alley's still open. I went there a few months ago," I said.

"Good. Let's all go bowling once the play is over."

"Cool," I said. I loved Dad's way of bowling, but I wished

I'd also let Mom teach me so I wouldn't embarrass myself with Zahara and Ally.

"Hi. I'm Zahara," Zahara said, smiling her big model smile.

"I know. You're in my math class. I mean, not that you're expected to know everyone who's in each of your classes. That's like thirty or thirty-five people times six classes." Could I possibly babble any more?

"Yeah, that's like a hundred ninety-five people," Zahara said, actually seeming interested.

I nodded. "Except some people are in more than one of your classes, right? So you'd have to subtract the duplicates. But, still, it's a lot. Start with a hundred eighty to two hundred ten people, or a hundred ninety-five on average like you said. Then subtract about . . ." Yes, I *could* possibly babble more. A lot more. I pressed my teeth together to shut myself up.

"I bet you get As in math," Ally said. She turned to Zahara. "Violet's really smart."

I shrugged. But I *did* get As in math. With Ms. Merriweather's supplemental stuff, I'd have to work for my A. But so far, I was really enjoying it.

"Sorry I didn't recognize you," Zahara said. "I'm awful

with faces. I think I might have this disease called face blind-ness I heard about last year. Or more like face nearsightedness or something. Plus, I hardly ever pay attention in math class."

"Zahara, this is Violet Summers," Ally said, because I'd been too busy blabbing about calculating math students to tell Zahara my name.

"Oh yeah," Zahara said. "You have a big part in the play, right?"

I nodded.

"My parents wouldn't let me try out. They said I shouldn't do acting unless I get paid for it." She sighed. "You're the Tin Man or the tiger or something?"

The tiger? If McKenzie heard that, she'd say Zahara was so dumb. When we saw her commercial, McKenzie had said, "You mean Orange County's *Worst* Ice Cream."

I gazed at McKenzie and caught her looking at me. She quickly stared down at her phone. Maybe she'd called it Orange County's Worst Ice Cream because she was jealous. She was probably jealous right now.

I turned away from her.

"The tiger?" Ally asked with a smile. "Zahara, there's no tiger in *The Wizard of Oz.*"

Zahara shrugged. "Lions and tigers and bears, oh my?"

"There's no bear either," Ally said.

They both laughed.

"Hey, can I sit with you guys?" I asked, which would have been a very brave thing to do if I hadn't been standing by their table for so long already.

"Oh yeah, sit," Ally said. "Sit, Miss Tiger."

"Or Miss Bear," Zahara said.

"Grr." I raised my hands and shaped them like bear claws.

We laughed together as I plopped down between them.

TWENTY-THREE

$\mathcal{M}$om drove me nuts the next morning. I couldn't even lie in bed after hitting my snooze button without her leaning over me, breathing her coffee breath on my face. I couldn't stand still after my shower and enjoy the warm steam without Mom calling out, "You'll be late for school!" I couldn't stare at my bedroom mirror while wearing my striped sweater and then my pink one and then my brown one and then my striped one again without Mom telling me to hurry up. And it was impossible to remember when I'd worn each sweater last and what jeans went best with them, because Mom's "Violet, come on!" made my brain go blank.

By the time we left for school, I didn't know who was madder: me or Mom. Probably Mom. Her eyes narrowed into slits like she was peering out of a Halloween mask. Her lips pressed together so tightly they made one thin line. She looked like she was constipated, though I wasn't dumb enough to point that out.

Just when I thought Mom was done telling me what to do, she said, "Put your seat belt on."

I sighed.

"Violet, you have to get ready for school faster," Mom said like she'd said a quadrillion times before.

"Okay, I will," I said for the quadrillionth time. Then I mumbled, "We're only a few minutes late."

Normally I'd text McKenzie something like, "Late. Don't wait for me." But McKenzie wouldn't be waiting for me anymore. Ally and I weren't good enough friends to wait for each other before school every day. Not yet, anyway.

"I'm tired of nagging you," Mom said, "believe it or not."

"Not," I muttered.

"So I thought about it, and I'm changing things up." Mom sounded cheery now. She let out a big breath. "I'm done waking you up or telling you to hurry or trying to rush you in the morning."

"Really? Is this an early Christmas gift?"

Mom flashed a smile. "A gift for both of us."

I smiled back at her. "Best gift ever! Thanks!"

"But there's a catch. From now on, if you're not in the car by seven forty-five, you walk to school."

I groaned. "That'll make me later than ever. Do you know how long it takes to walk to school?"

"Twenty minutes or so."

"Yeah. And what if I have a big thing to carry, like that history class project?"

"Then you'd better make sure to get ready for school on time." Mom flashed another smile.

I did not smile back. "If I have too many tardies, I'll get detention."

"That'll be your problem, not mine," Mom said.

"I can't get detention! I have rehearsals every day after school."

Mom shrugged. "Well, it's up to you. I guess you should get yourself ready on time."

I glared at her. "I guess *you* should get me a real Christmas present. Because this one stinks."

π

Voicemail from Violet:

"Hi, McKenzie. It's me. Obviously. I saw you looking at me in the cafeteria today. And you saw me looking at you. Do you want to sit with me at lunch tomorrow? I mean, with me and Ally and whoever else joins the table. Ally's nice. We shouldn't be scared to try new things. I'm not saying you're scared. But I'm not saying you're *not* scared either. You know? Give me a call, okay? We don't even have to talk that much about my dad. Or about that kick at lunch. And maybe your mom. I wish we *could* talk about that stuff though. Okay, well, I miss you."

π

It had been two days since I'd left the voicemail. McKenzie hadn't called me back or texted or sat with me at lunch. I missed her. I worried about her too. We only had mothers to look out for us now, and I didn't think McKenzie's mother looked out for her too well.

The day before, I saw her eating with three girls I didn't know very well: Darcy Bollinger, Pearl something, and a girl named either Maddy or Megan or Molly or Jane. I doubted McKenzie knew those girls very well either.

Maybe McKenzie had decided to be generous and give those girls a second chance, like I'd done with Ally, and Ally had done with me. I was willing to give McKenzie a second chance, but she didn't seem to want it. What she really seemed to want was lunch company that wasn't me.

Today was only the third day Ally and I were eating together, but she'd put her backpack and a notebook on the bench across from her to save spots for Zahara and me.

Ally must have seen me looking at McKenzie as I walked over, because she said, "Did McKenzie ever tell you why she's mad at me?"

I sat down. "McKenzie's not mad at you. Maybe jealous."

"No, she's mad." Ally said softly, "She didn't tell you about the hand-me-downs?"

I shook my head.

"Last year, I . . ." Ally's voice got so soft I had to lean in close to hear. "Well, I noticed her clothes weren't in very good shape. And I get a ton of hand-me-downs from my mom's boss's daughter. Really my grandmother's boss's daughter, but I call my grandmother 'Mom.' Anyway, I'm too tall for a lot of the clothes, so I offered McKenzie some of them."

"That was nice of you," I said. Nicer than I had been. I hadn't even thought about giving McKenzie clothes until my mom had bought some for her. I hoped Mom would keep buying her stuff.

"McKenzie didn't consider it nice," Ally said. "She considered it insulting. I made the offer in private, but I probably didn't say it right."

"Say what right?" Zahara asked as she sat next to me.

"Oh. Nothing." I grabbed my sandwich and bit into it.

"Nothing," Ally said. "And speaking of nothing, let me show you something."

"How could nothing lead you to something? They're like inverse functions of each other," Zahara said.

I gaped at Zahara. Wasn't *inverse functions* a math term?

"Here it is." Ally handed me her phone. A picture of a boy filled the screen. He looked a little older than us, and had pale skin, short hair, and big ears. Ally said, "This is my cousin Cameron at his Boy Scout awards ceremony."

"Congratulations?" I said like a question.

"Cameron's really proud of that picture," she said. "He got an award for most passionate. Or most *com*passionate. Something like that."

I had no idea where she was going with this. I raised my eyebrows at her, meaning *SOS*.

"There's this big, stupid rumor about me," Ally said,

which did not seem to Save Our Ship, but rather to knock a big hole into it.

"You've probably heard about Ally dating a ninth-grader," Zahara said.

I didn't know whether to lie or not. I glanced McKenzie's way as if *she* could Save Our Ship. She was staring at Pearl, who was talking with her mouth full of food. Yuck.

"That rumor is fake," Ally said. "I'm not dating an older boy. I've never dated anyone. My cousin and I hang out. Someone must have seen us together."

Guilt globbed inside me. My stomach felt like it did after eating too many Slab o' Ribs at Bonzo's Barbecue.

"Stupid rumor," Zahara said.

"Yeah," I said as the glob of guilt grew.

"So stupid," Zahara said. "I met Ally's cousin once. All he did was talk about his merit badges. The only boy I would date would be . . ." She leaned across the table and whispered, "Braden Chalmers. Mr. Muscles!"

I tried to hide my disgust. Braden ate everything with his hands and looked like a blond-haired boulder. He wasn't any-where near as cute as Diego Ortiz.

This week Diego and I had spent Saturday and every day

after school together in rehearsals, but mostly in character onstage. The play was only a week away.

"I know who you'd date, Violet," Ally said. She whispered, "Diego Ortiz."

"What? Me?" I felt my face get warm. "Diego?"

Ally nodded. "Your face is as red as a throbbing heart. I've suspected your crush since the first rehearsal. I always hear you laughing harder than anyone at Diego's jokes."

"Just because I think he's funny doesn't mean I have a crush on—"

"But you do," Ally said smugly. "And I'm pretty sure he likes you, too."

$$\pi$$

Wishful arithmetic:

Violet + Diego = Sitting in a tree, k-i-s-s-i-n-g.

TWENTY-FOUR

I had Mom drop me off at rehearsal on Saturday at nine o'clock sharp—an hour before rehearsal really started. As soon as Mom left, I did too.

I walked quickly. I needed to get to McKenzie's house, try to make up with her, and return to the school auditorium on time. I also walked quickly because I was a little scared. If Mom had known what I was doing, she'd probably be scared for me.

We had picked up McKenzie at her house a lot, but seeing the houses flash by from the car window at twenty-five miles per hour was different than looking at them from the sidewalk at three miles per hour. Some of the homes in McKenzie's neighborhood were cute. If my mom were selling them, she'd call them "hidden gems." But most of the homes I passed could, at best, be described as "cozy," "charming," or "quaint." Some of them couldn't be called any of those things. With their faded paint, dirty windows, and dead yards, the best term for them was "handyman special" or "a steal for investors."

McKenzie's house was the worst one of all. It would have to be called a "tear down," meaning it was such a disaster that the entire house would have to be torn down and replaced.

I stood on the sidewalk for a minute, staring at the cracked, stained driveway, the peeling paint, the front window with duct tape over it. My body felt heavy as cement.

I made myself walk forward, stepping over ancient brown and green hoses that lay jumbled along the narrow path to the front door. Lying on the cement around the door were rusted bike parts, a huge toaster, and a broken umbrella.

I knocked on the door.

"Go away!" McKenzie's mom said loudly in her raspy voice.

Before I could convince myself to leave, I said squeakily, "Is McKenzie home? It's me, Violet."

"The Girl Scout?" McKenzie's mom asked.

"Yes. I mean, no. Not anymore." I called out, "McKenzie? Are you there? I came here to—"

McKenzie cracked open the front door. She didn't look happy to see me. More like nervous. Her lips were pursed, and she crossed one arm over her chest. She was wearing the old gray nightgown, her sleepover uniform. "What are you doing here? Did your mom drive you?" Her gaze darted over my shoulder to the street.

"No, I walked here. My mom doesn't know." Right then I wished my mom knew. I wished she were standing right next to me.

"Get out of here!" McKenzie whispered, sounding panicked.

I whispered back, "But I just—"

McKenzie's mother flung open the front door. She wore a faded red bathrobe and looked shorter than I remembered, probably because I'd grown taller. She had large, dark eyes like McKenzie's. But while McKenzie's eyes always seemed to shine with energy, the shine in her mother's eyes looked like pure anger.

"You're trespassing," Ms. Williston barked. McKenzie had said her mom was still really sad from McKenzie's dad dying, but to me she just seemed mad.

A smell hit me. It reminded me of the dumpster near the

school auditorium. I looked inside the house, but couldn't see very far in. There was a large cardboard box with random stuff like electrical cords and old towels spilling out of it, a three-legged chair, an old pizza box, a cracked computer monitor, and a pile of ratty winter coats no one would wear in Orange County—or probably anywhere else.

"Did your mother send you?" McKenzie's mom asked like an accusation.

I shook my head.

"I know she called the social worker about me and that ridiculous volunteer group. She needs to butt out of my life."

I didn't know my mom had butted in. But if my mom had called people to help McKenzie and her mom, then, well, it seemed like she had good reason to.

"Get out, Violet!" McKenzie whispered. Now she sounded desperate.

I stared at the train wreck of her house. It was rude and it was making me nauseous, but I couldn't help it. I couldn't look away or speak or move.

"Please!" McKenzie hissed, either to me or her mother.

Then McKenzie's mother did us all a big favor and slammed the door shut.

For a few seconds I stood, still frozen, in front of the dusty, dirty door.

Then I turned and ran.

Running is the last thing you should do when your stomach hurts. But the faster I got away from McKenzie's house, the better I felt.

I wondered whether McKenzie felt the same way whenever Mom picked her up in old but pristine Grandpa Falls-Apart and took her to our clean, orderly house. I wondered how McKenzie had put up with my stupid complaints about Mom nagging Dad to stop cluttering our hallway with his shoes.

I stopped running about a block from school and tried to calm down before rehearsal. I sang the Cowardly Lion's Courage song in my head. It took about a dozen repeated verses before my breathing returned to normal.

But the stink of McKenzie's house still came through every pore in my body.

Text to McKenzie: R U ok?

McKenzie: Don't ever tell anyone about my mom or my house

Violet: ☹

McKenzie: Don't tell anyone

McKenzie: Promise me

Violet: I won't tell. I promise. R U ok tho?

McKenzie: Fine. Don't ever mention it!!!

Violet: Do U want help?

McKenzie: Don't ever mention it

Violet: Ok I won't ☹

TWENTY-FIVE

$\mathscr{F}$ive days after going to McKenzie's house, my stomach was churning again, but for a different reason: We were about to begin our first and only dress rehearsal.

I stood with most of the cast in the crowded greenroom, watching a video monitor of the stage. Ally stood upstage in her Dorothy costume—a polyester white blouse and gingham dress that Mr. Goldstein had snagged online, and red clogs her mom/grandma had heaped with glitter. Next to Ally were Jada Morales, who played Auntie Em, and Henry Tomaselli, who conveniently played Uncle Henry. The music teacher played a medley of songs from *The Wizard of Oz* on the piano.

Mr. Goldstein sat in the front row with his husband, who was skinnier than him and had even less hair. Seated around them were about ten really old people from the senior center where Mr. Goldstein's husband worked as the activities director. Principal Slimeball (real name: Principal Simon) sat a few rows back. At an assembly last year, she said we should each give 110 percent to making middle school count, which made me lose all respect for her, since giving anything over 100 percent is a mathematical impossibility.

Ms. Merriweather sat near the back, but her height and magenta hair made her stand out. I didn't want to mess up in front of her, not after she'd written on my last homework packet that I should think seriously about a career in math. I also didn't want to disappoint any of the senior citizens, because this could be the last play they saw before they died.

Diego was sitting on the folding chair right next to me, with our knees almost touching. The thing Ally had said— "I'm pretty sure he likes you, too"—whooshed inside my head along with a quadrillion other thoughts.

SOME OF THE QUADRILLION THOUGHTS WHOOSHING IN MY HEAD

Does Diego really like me?

Like *like* me?

How does Ally know, especially since she hasn't even dated anyone?

217

Why would the funniest guy in school like someone whose jokes are about as funny as Ally's little
sisters' knock-knock jokes?

Fortunately, makeup covered my blushing cheeks. Unfor-

tunately, it was thick, greasy, gold makeup. It matched my big,

furry gold costume and the hood of gold yarn over my head.

Not a good look for me. Plus, I smelled bad. I probably stank.

The last person who wore this costume must have run a mar-

athon in it.

Diego smelled fine, but he wasn't exactly looking his best

either. He wore silver makeup, a silver shirt, weird silver pants,

and a papier-mâché hat fastened to his head with a quadrillion

bobby pins. He was supposed to be a Tin Man with an oilcan

on his head, but he looked more like a disco robot wearing a

dunce cap. I still thought he was cute.

On the video monitor, the right half of the faded red stage

curtain opened. About ten seconds later, the left half started

to jerk. It took another thirty seconds or so for it to open all

the way.

"Yikes," I said.

Ally uttered her first line, "Auntie M&M!"

A soft groan went through the greenroom.

"Auntie M&M and Uncle Oh Henry Bar," Diego whispered.

I very cleverly responded with another "Yikes." I hoped Ally wasn't freaking out too much about her mistake.

Mr. Goldstein had told us the show must go on no matter what. If someone forgot a prop or a line, we were supposed to improvise so the mistake wouldn't be obvious to the audience. But no one could hide the fact that Dorothy had called her aunt "M&M." Especially not after Jada/Auntie Em/Auntie M&M started laughing.

The prop guy ran onstage and handed Ally a basket with a stuffed dog in it, which she should have been holding when the curtain opened.

Ally ad-libbed the line, "Tonto!" Then she covered her mouth, uncovered it, and said, "I mean Toto."

Jada bent over with laughter. The white powder on her hair flew all over the place and made her sneeze. Her sneeze sent more powder into the air, which made Henry/Uncle Henry sneeze.

Backstage, Diego whispered, "Is this *The Wizard of Oz* or *The Wizard of Schnoz*?"

"Yikes," was my witty comeback again.

Behind us, Sarah Blanchette said, "Ally is screwing up so bad."

"Give her a break," I said at the same time Diego said, "Leave her alone."

We stared into each other's eyes as if to say by ESP, *We are on the exact same wavelength, joining together to fight evil, like soulmate superheroes.*

Ally made up for her flubbed lines by singing "Somewhere over the Rainbow" beautifully.

After Ally's solo, one of the really old ladies said loudly, "Like a taller Judy Garland."

Then a really old man said equally loudly, "Thelma, simmer down."

Then Thelma (most likely) said, "Shut your pie-hole, Jerome."

Mr. Goldstein's husband made a loud shushing sound.

The play didn't improve. Two Munchkins (Henry's and Diego's younger brothers) ran into each other and fell on their butts. Another Munchkin (Mr. Goldstein's niece) got clobbered by Glinda the Good Witch's wand. Sarah Blanchette's Scarecrow rope belt came untied, so she sang "If I Only

Had a Brain" while one of her hands clutched the top of her burlap pants.

"Poor dear is losing her slacks," Thelma said, and Mr. Goldstein's husband loudly shushed her again.

I messed up too, skipping a verse of my "Courage" song and, later, tripping over the melted witch, who came back to life for a second to say "Ow."

Diego's bobby pins kept flying off his head. Toward the end, his oilcan/dunce cap fell off. He said with a smile, "That was meant to happen."

No one laughed—not even me.

HORRIFYING DISASTERS IN U.S. HISTORY

1. The Great San Francisco Fire

2. The Donner cannibalism party

3. The sinking of the *Titanic*

4. Horton Johnson Middle School's production of *The Wizard of Oz*

The dress rehearsal seemed to last a quadrillion years. During this era, I thought about how I could skip out on the actual play. If only I hadn't used up all my dead relative excuses! If only Mr. Goldstein hadn't kept saying the show must go on. My hopes turned to faking a serious-but-temporary disease or injury.

Disease or Injury	Seriousness Level	Able to Get out of the Play?	Problems
Cold	1	No	Have to fake sneeze and cough, which Diego might find gross.
Stomach Flu	3	No	Diego would definitely find vomiting gross.
Sprained Ankle	3	No	Have to fake a limp.
Broken Limb	4	No	Might be stuck wearing a cast for six weeks.
Two Broken Limbs	6	No	Mr. Goldstein might push me onstage in a wheelchair and make me sing "If I only had a working arm and leg."

Finally, we reached the last scene. Ally said her famous "no place like home" line and clicked her heels three times. In rehearsal, Mr. Goldstein had told her to click with exuberance and gusto, and she did.

Her left clog flew into the air.

"Heads up!" Ms. Merriweather exclaimed.

I let out a sigh as the curtain shakily closed and the horror finally ended.

Mr. Goldstein called everyone to the stage. Our faces looked shocked, like we'd barely survived an apocalypse. Mr. Goldstein seemed pretty shocked himself. But he said, "Let's give a big round of applause to everyone for trying so hard and braving the dress rehearsal." He started clapping.

No one joined in.

He stopped after about six claps. "All right. Down to business. Stage manager, we must repair the curtain. Ally, be careful when you click your heels. Your ruby slipper just missed one of the senior citizens in our audience and glitter-bombed several people in the second row."

Ally was stooped over, hugging her arms across her chest. This rehearsal had to be worse for her than anyone else. She had screwed up first and last and in between, appeared in practically every scene, and had no confidence in her ability to remember her lines.

I walked over to her and squeezed her arm.

She looked at me and sighed.

"They say the worse the dress rehearsal, the better the actual show," I whispered.

"Really?" she asked, a microscopic speck of hope in her voice.

I nodded. I hoped Ally didn't ask who "they" were and where I'd heard that, because "they" was really me and I'd made it all up. Also, it was as logical as saying the worse you did on a practice test, the better you'd do on the actual test, or the worse your parents' marriage was, the better their chances of reuniting. But I'd lie to Ally all night if it would cheer her up.

Mr. Goldstein spent the next few minutes giving us notes. He finished by saying, "Let's not dwell on our mistakes. Hang up your costumes, put away the props, and rest well tonight. Curtain call tomorrow is at six p.m. Onward. And break a leg." He tried but failed to smile, shook his head, and walked off.

I hurried backstage, got out of the disgustingly sweaty Lion costume and scrubbed the greasepaint from my face.

Back in my school clothes, I walked through the cursed auditorium and empty seats. They'd be filled tomorrow as we performed our disaster in front of my mom and other parents and teachers and hundreds of kids from school.

If I couldn't get a serious-but-temporary injury or disease, my best hope was for a large house to soar through the sky before showtime and flatten the auditorium.

TWENTY-SIX

When Mom picked me up, she didn't even ask how the dress rehearsal went. Instead, as soon as I got in Grandpa Falls-Apart, she gushed, "I did it! We closed escrow!"

I knew from hearing Mom talk over the years that "closing escrow" means a deal is final—no changing your mind and returning a house for something better. It's good news for real estate agents, but the way Mom was going on about the open houses and showings and negotiating she did, you'd think no one had ever sold a house before. I hadn't heard her this happy since before Dad left. Actually, I hadn't heard her this happy when Dad was home. Even though we sat inches from each other in the car, her cheer was not contagious.

"This is a game changer," Mom said as if she'd closed escrow on the Empire State Building.

I felt an urge to punch something, but I choked out, "Congratulations."

"Violet? Did something happen? How was the dress rehearsal?" Mom had lost her annoying perkiness, which should have made me feel better but didn't.

I looked out the car window, even though it was too dark to see anything. "Rehearsal was fine."

"Was that a great 'fine,' a good 'fine,' or a terrible 'fine'?"

I didn't answer.

"Because you'd probably say rehearsal was fine if a lightning bolt destroyed the auditorium."

"I wish," I muttered.

Mom put her hand on my shoulder. "That bad?"

"It was fine. Terribly fine." I let out a laugh that sounded like a hysterical bark.

"Someone forgot their lines?" Mom asked.

"Not just someone. Lots of people forgot their lines. And their cues. And their props. And their brains."

"Isn't that part of the play? The Scarecrow forgetting she has brains?"

"Yeah, but it wasn't only the Scarecrow."

"Oh no." Mom sighed, almost as if it had been *her* dress rehearsal that had gone so wrong. "What happened?"

I told her. Maybe it was because she seemed so concerned or maybe because there was no one else to talk to about it—since McKenzie and I weren't speaking, Dad was pretending he wasn't a father, and I couldn't add to Ally's suffering—but it felt good to tell Mom about the dress rehearsal. I described the Aunty M&M and Toto/Tonto mistakes, my stinky Lion costume, Diego tripping over the yellow brick road and ad-libbing, "I'm filing a lawsuit," and the Wicked Witch's hiccupping fit. I couldn't tell Mom everything that went wrong. The car ride wasn't long enough. We'd probably need to drive cross-country for that.

Every so often, Mom said "Wow" or "Oh gee" or "Sheesh." She also said, "That Diego sounds like he has a great sense of humor."

"He's pretty funny," I said as casually as possible. The one thing I would never, ever, ever tell Mom about was my crush on Diego.

Mom acted so calm that I felt a little less worried by the end of the car ride. What had seemed to me like an endless, nightmarish disaster probably seemed to her like a bumpy few hours. In fact, when I told her about one of the monkeys accidentally wearing her costume backward with the tail in front, Mom did a fake cough like she was covering up a laugh.

Spilling my guts (some of them, anyway) to Mom had been a good move on my part. Though I wasn't going to do it on a regular basis or anything.

As we walked into the house, Mom draped her arm around me and said, "There's an old saying: Bad dress, good show. That means a bad dress rehearsal is a sign of a good opening night."

I shook my head. "Good try at a pep talk, Mom. But that's not a real thing."

"Yes, it is. It's a common theater expression, like 'break a leg.'"

I stopped walking. "Seriously?"

"Seriously," Mom said.

"Bad dress rehearsals lead to good opening nights?"

Mom raised her eyebrows. "Honestly, it sounds a bit silly to me. But it's a common saying."

"It sounds ridiculous to me," I said. I'd thought I was lying to Ally when I'd told her that. But if it was a real expression, maybe there was some truth behind it. If opening nights came out the opposite of dress rehearsals, then we would have the best opening night ever.

While Mom microwaved our dinner, I sent Ally a text:

Violet: Remember bad dress rehearsal means great opening night

Ally: My dad said that too. Sounds crazy

Violet: Maybe not. And remember the theme of *Wizard of Oz*

Ally: There's no place like home

Violet: No, what Goldstein said. Find what's been inside u all along and use it

Ally: Oh yeah

Violet: Find ur talent and what u yearn for and use them opening night

Ally: I'm scared I'll mess up again and ruin the play for everyone

Violet: U cant ruin it for me no matter what. Best thing about this play was becoming ur friend

Ally: ❤

Violet: ❤

π

As I heaped mashed potatoes onto my plate that night, Mom pointed to the glass bowl of green beans on the table and said, "You know the rule," meaning I had to eat a vegetable at dinner.

"Okay." I speared a single green bean and dropped it on my plate.

"You must be looking forward to more free time once your play is over."

"Uh-huh," I grunted. But free time meant not hanging out with Ally and Diego and the other actors every day. I wasn't looking forward to that. My mom didn't know me at all.

"Though maybe you'll miss being with your theater friends every day," Mom said.

Okay, maybe she knew me a little.

"I'd like to talk to you about Thanksgiving," Mom said.

Every Thanksgiving, my family—what used to be my family—drove to Fresno. We always stayed a couple of nights at my grandparents' house. They had a nice, 2,600-square-foot colonial-style home, plus a quarter-acre backyard that was gigantic by Orange County standards.

Most of my dad's family lived in Fresno, so there were lots

of relatives there—my Uncle Nate and Aunt Amber and their three boys, my great-aunt and great-uncle and great-grandma, and a few second cousins or cousins once removed or something like that.

Mom spent most of her time helping Grandma cook and wash dishes, listening to stories about Dad as a boy, and wearing a tiny fake smile. Dad and Uncle Nate always drank a lot on Thanksgiving. It was another thing my parents fought about, on the drive up and on the drive down and sometimes randomly during the year. Dad said Mom was the only person who couldn't even relax on Thanksgiving. Mom said it was supposed to be *Thanks*giving, not *Dranks*giving.

Mom interrupted my thoughts. "I can call your grandparents and ask if we're welcome there. If you want to come, they probably wouldn't say no."

"Will Dad be there?" I asked, pouring ketchup on my potatoes, fish sticks, and green bean.

"I don't know." Mom put down her fork and stared at me.

Was driving five hours to Fresno and listening to Dad's voice get louder and slurrier worth it just for the chance to see him? Was anything worth the chance to see Dad? There was my Aunt Amber's caramel-apple pie to think about. Last Thanksgiving, Dad and I each ate a big slice for dessert, another slice a few hours later, and a third slice for breakfast.

Thanksgiving was supposed to be about being with all your family—your mother *and* father. But if Dad couldn't even bother to drive a few miles to see me, why should I have to go up to Fresno to see him get drunk with his relatives?

"If you want," Mom said, "we can do something else for Thanksgiving this year."

"Okay, let's skip Fresno," I said, surprising myself with my eagerness.

Mom started to smile, but stopped herself. She said, "I was thinking we could still go away for the weekend, maybe fly up to San Francisco."

I glared at her across the table. "You only know I want to fly to San Francisco because you read my private emails to Dad."

"I'm sorry. I never should have done that." She picked at the cuticle on her ringless ring finger.

"Anyway, I wanted to go on vacation with you and *Dad*. Not just with you," I said.

"I wanted that too." Mom sounded yearn-y.

I stared at her jagged cuticle and wondered if she'd checked her phone and emails a quadrillion times a day like I had, hoping for Dad to say he'd made a huge mistake.

"But we're not going back to how we used to be," Mom said. "And it's better for your dad and me to move on than to keep fighting with each other."

I nodded. I knew that now. It had taken me a while, but I had finally, sadly, faced up to it.

"How about just you and me?" Mom asked. "We could stay in a hotel. Maybe eat clam chowder in sourdough bread bowls and ride a cable car and go to a museum."

"I don't get it," I said. "Last time we went to San Francisco, we drove there and stayed in that old motel in Oakland and took the subway in, because you said hotels in San Francisco were too expensive. Dad said the stains on the motel carpet looked like blood."

"They might have been wine stains," Mom said. "Things have picked up for us financially. Once that deal went through—"

"What deal?" I smothered a fish stick in ketchup and ate it.

"The house I sold in Laguna Beach. I've been talking to you about it for months."

Ugh. Real estate talk. I took a long drink of water to keep myself awake.

"It's not just a house, it's a mansion," Mom went on, "I priced it at three and a half million dollars."

I had a coughing fit. Water shot out of my mouth and nose.

Mom laughed. "It sold for less than three and a half million, Violet."

I wiped my face with a napkin.

"The buyer bid it down to three point two million."

I let out a smaller cough. Real estate agents get paid three percent of the sales price. Three percent of $3.2 million is $96,000. Whoa!

"My share of the sales price is very nice," Mom said.

"Very nice? It's fantastic!"

"It really is." Mom grinned. "And now the couple across the street wants me to sell their home too."

Cha-ching! "Tell me more!"

"The square-footage isn't as big, but apparently the kitchen was recently renovated, walls down and everything, to open up the space. They put in a Viking stove, induction oven . . ."

I ate my mashed potatoes while Mom rambled on about travertine flooring and subway tiles and wainscoting, whatever those were.

Things Mom Wants to Do in San Francisco

Eat authentic Asian cuisine, like gross raw fish

Go to the art museum

See a play

Things I Want to Do in San Francisco

Eat hot fudge sundaes in Ghirardelli Square

Go to the celebrity wax museum

Never set foot in a theater again

Even if I didn't get to eat hot fudge sundaes or go to the celebrity wax museum, I bet the trip was going to be awesome.

TWENTY-SEVEN

As I sat across from Ally at lunch the next day, she let out a big yawn.

"I'm excited to see you too," I said.

She clapped her hand over her mouth. "I'm sorry. I couldn't sleep last night."

I could tell. Ally's eyes were red, and her face was paler than usual. Shockingly, she looked less than beautiful today. Of course, she still looked pretty.

I leaned across the lunch table and put my hand on her arm. "You're going to do great tonight. We all will."

She shook her head. "The only chance I have to get through lunch and the rest of the day without crying is to not talk about the play."

I nodded, secretly grateful I didn't have to give another pep talk. I did not feel peppy.

"Let's talk about something else, like . . ." Ally stared past me.

I turned around. McKenzie was walking toward us, wearing the red T-shirt and Levi's my mom had bought her, and carrying her lunch bag.

She stopped in front of our table and said, "Hi," as casually as if we'd traveled back in time, before McKenzie had kicked me, before I'd told her I liked Ally, before Ally had taped the note on my locker, before Mr. Goldstein posted the cast list, before we tried out for the play, to the time when everything was simple, before my dad left.

Had everything been simple though? Even if none of that stuff had happened, other things would have. Other things already had. Deep inside, I'd been mad at McKenzie for talking me into quitting Girl Scouts. And I was mad at myself for letting myself get talked into it. And there was that argument between our moms before the campout. I had never asked McKenzie about her mother. I'd told myself it wasn't polite, but really it was easier not to bring it up. With all the silent stuff that had gone on between us, our friendship had been as shaky as the stage curtain. It had never been simple. You could barely even make sense of it in a graph or chart.

COMPLICATIONS IN FRIENDSHIP
WITH McKENZIE

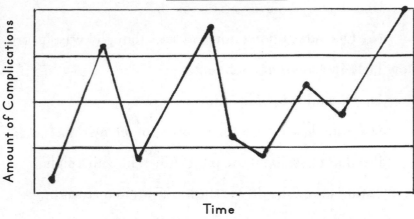

Amount of Complications

Time

"Um, wow. McKenzie," Ally said, not even pretending to act casual. "Violet? Violet, why aren't you saying anything?"

Because my mouth was hanging open.

"Do you want to sit with us?" Ally asked.

"Violet?" McKenzie asked, saying my name like a question.

It sounded strange. She never said my name like a question. Before, her "Violet" had been more like an order. She'd lost her confidence, or at least her display of it. What if the confidence I'd gained in the last few weeks had been stolen from McKenzie? But confidence was a variable, not a fixed number. It could increase inside me without decreasing inside anyone else.

"You don't mind if I sit with you?" McKenzie asked.

I nodded.

"Does that nod mean you do mind?"

"No. Of course I don't mind," I said, though I wasn't sure how I felt. I wasn't *that* confident.

"Please, sit down," Ally said.

McKenzie slowly sat at the empty spot on my right.

"Just don't talk about the play," Ally said with a sigh.

"I heard about the dress rehearsal," McKenzie said.

Had she come here to gloat? I wouldn't let her. If she said one mean word, I'd tell her off. I'd remind her that at least Ally and I had stuck with the play instead of dropping out before the first rehearsal. Ally and I would be laughingstocks, but we'd be brave laughingstocks.

McKenzie shrugged. "I thought maybe if you needed something . . . Help with practicing your lines or . . ." She wasn't gloating at all. She was being nice.

"Thanks. But the best way to help me now is to not mention the P.L.A.Y.," Ally said.

"I know what you can do, McKenzie," I said. "Tell a joke to distract us from the you-know-what. You're really funny."

"People keep saying I'm funny." She grinned. "Funny looking."

I forced a giggle.

"McKenzie, you're not funny looking," Ally said. "Not at all."

"I was joking." McKenzie crossed her arms, probably thinking Ally was doing her sweet act again. She didn't know it wasn't just an act.

"I got the joke," I said.

"Here's something else funny." McKenzie leaned forward and whispered, "Bella Perez tried to cut her own bangs and botched it. Now they're more like wisps than bangs."

"I don't think it's funny to insult people," Ally said.

I didn't either. I never really did. But I used to laugh at McKenzie's whispered insults anyway and add my own insults right back.

"What are you, Ally? The humor police?" McKenzie asked, sounding mad.

Ally didn't answer. She looked at me and raised her eyebrows as if to say *She's your friend, not mine. Deal with it.* Or maybe I was just imagining that.

McKenzie crossed her arms. "Violet asked me to be funny, so I was."

Now *she* was blaming me too.

But McKenzie had made a peace offering by coming to our table today. It was up to me to keep the peace. So I said, "McKenzie, you won't believe what my mom just did." I wanted to change the subject, but also I was dying to talk about it. "She sold a mansion."

"That three-and-a-half-million-dollar house in Laguna Beach with the tennis court?" McKenzie asked.

"Uh-huh," I said. "How did you know about that?"

"How could I not? Your mom was always talking about it."

She was? I hadn't even known about the tennis court. I wondered if McKenzie understood what wainscoting was too. I'd thought of her as self-centered, but I was the one who'd ignored my own mother.

"I helped your mom with an open house for that place. It really is a mansion," McKenzie said.

"You? What? She took you to an open house?"

McKenzie blushed. "Your mom's sort of teaching me the real estate biz."

I thought about the clothes Mom had bought for McKenzie, the social worker and volunteer group Mom had sent to her home, all the times Mom had driven her to our house and made dinner for her and let her sleep over. Dad wasn't really part of our family anymore, but McKenzie was.

"So did that house close escrow?" she asked, sounding as eager as if it were her house, or her mom.

I nodded.

"What's escrow?" Ally asked.

"It means when a sale becomes final, like a done deal," McKenzie said. "I knew Violet's mom could sell that mansion. She's the best."

"Except when she's nagging or asking me a quadrillion questions," I said.

McKenzie shrugged.

Ally frowned.

I wished I could take back what I'd just said. My mom was there for me, unlike Ally's mom or McKenzie's. I wasn't sure why McKenzie's mother hardly ever drove her places and stored all that junk in her house, whether she was despondent about her husband dying or had some kind of mental illness. Once McKenzie and I were by ourselves, I needed to get up my nerve and ask her about it.

Not only was my mom a lot better than McKenzie's and

Ally's mothers, she was better than she used to be. She'd quit nagging me. Sort of, anyway. She still had slipups. But if I ever made a Mom Situations from Bad to Worst list, like the one I'd done for dads, my mom wouldn't even qualify for the list. She'd be on a Mom Situations from Good to Great list.

Though she wouldn't be the greatest mom. That spot would go to Lindsey Rodriguez-Smith's mother, who managed the ten-plex theater in the mall. Lindsey got to see every movie there for free and buy popcorn and candy for half off. She'd seen *Wonder Woman* eight times.

"So how much commission did your mom earn on that mansion?" McKenzie asked. Before I could answer, she said, "Ally, real estate agents get three percent of the selling price. Violet can figure out the exact number because she's, like, a math genius."

Ally nodded.

"No, I'm not," I said, wondering if I was. "It sold for three point two million, so her commission is ninety-six thousand dollars."

"Minus a third of that for the company your mom works for," McKenzie said.

"Really?"

"Yeah. That's what your mom said."

"Too bad. So, two-thirds of 96,000 is 64,000." My tone was casual, but inside I felt an excited jolt from all the money we'd get.

"I can't believe how fast you figured that out in your head," Ally said, gazing wide-eyed at me.

I tried not to smile.

"Told you she was a math genius," McKenzie said. "I would have needed a calculator and about an hour."

"Me too. And I probably would have gotten it wrong," Ally said.

"Violet may be a math genius, but she can't do this." McKenzie touched her tongue to her nose.

Ally and I laughed, tried it, failed, and laughed again. Some color had come back to Ally's face, though her eyes still looked tired.

"But can you guys do this?" Ally made a fart noise with her underarm. Over our laughter, she said, "My little sisters taught me."

"Teach me. I'm so doing that in class," McKenzie said.

We practiced fart noises. We didn't even stop when Zahara Khalil came by with a couple of other girls. They shook their heads at us, but they were smiling. Ally was so popular she could even make fake farts seem cool. Though her popularity was based more on her niceness to everyone than on being cool. Plus, I bet even Ally would lose popularity points if she spent every lunch period making fart noises. There was probably a hard limit on that of, like, no more than twice a month. For girls, anyway. Boys seemed to have no limits on their love of anything involving farts.

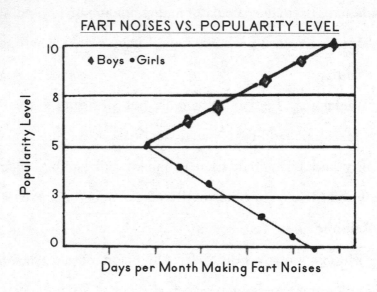

FART NOISES VS. POPULARITY LEVEL

♦ Boys ● Girls

Popularity Level

Days per Month Making Fart Noises

When the bell rang, I hated that lunch period was over. And it wasn't just because next period I had a quiz I hadn't studied for about a chapter I hadn't read in a textbook I'd barely opened. It was because of my new friend sitting across from me and my old friend sitting next to me, and the three of us laughing as if we'd always been happy together.

None of us got up from the lunch table until the cafeteria manager, McSneerface (not sure what her real name is), yelled, "Out, girls! Out!"

As we all stood, Ally said, "I hope you sit here next week too, McKenzie."

"Me too," I said. "Except Ally and I might not be here next week. After tonight's show, we might get expelled for ruining the school's reputation."

"I thought we weren't supposed to talk about the P.L.A.Y.," McKenzie said.

"It's okay," Ally said. "Violet might want to. She's just as freaked out as I am."

Judging from Ally's reddish eyes, I doubted that.

"You're going to do fine," McKenzie said flatly, avoiding our eyes. Obviously, McKenzie wasn't good at pep talks. She was not a peppy person in general.

"They say, 'Bad dress, good show,'" I said, attempting my own pep talk. "So our bad dress rehearsal means we'll put on a good show."

McKenzie raised her eyebrows.

"It makes no sense to me either," Ally said.

I shook my head. "Me neither."

The three of us exchanged small, sad smiles.

$$\pi$$

In class a few minutes later, I opened the pocket of my backpack to get a pen. That's how I found the note. I was so distracted at lunch, worrying about the play and about Ally and McKenzie sharing a table, that I didn't notice Zahara Khalil had unzipped my backpack pocket and slipped in a piece of notebook paper.

> *Hey, Violet,*
>
> *I realized something kind of cool/kind of dorky this morning in math class: You're the other person secretly doing supplemental work! Now it all adds up. (Pun intended.) Let's get together and talk numbers! Here's mine: 555-4790.*
>
> *Good luck with the play.*
>
> *Zahara*

TWENTY-EIGHT

I hadn't studied chaos theory yet, but if it involves frenzied masses, I was experiencing it . . . in the greenroom before the play.

Mr. Goldstein stood in the middle of the room, speaking loudly into his cell phone: "Kimmi, I'm sorry about your stress hives and your scary monkey nightmare. But you need to toughen up, get to school, and put on your Wicked Witch costume!"

Ally sat in the back corner, slumped over a highlighted script as she muttered her lines. Every ten seconds or so, she let out a long sigh.

Jian Cho, our props manager, burst into the greenroom. "Where's Toto?" he shouted. "We're toast without Toto!"

Ally looked up from her script and cried, "Toto's missing? Oh no!"

Sarah Blanchette walked into the greenroom with her mother.

"Parents are not permitted backstage," Mr. Goldstein said sternly.

"But Henry Tomaselli's father is here," she said.

"He's a mechanic. He's trying to fix the stage curtain. The entire right side won't even open!" He took a deep breath. "Mrs. Blanchette, find a seat in the audience. Please."

"Sarah needs my TLC," she said.

"TLC?" Diego murmured a few feet away. "Treatment Like a Child?"

I giggled, mostly from nerves.

Ally's grandmother walked into the greenroom.

Mr. Goldstein repeated, "Parents are not permitted backstage."

Ally's grandfather followed her, carrying three large pizza boxes.

"Never mind. Come in," Mr. Goldstein said.

My phone pinged with a text.

McKenzie: Can't wait to see the show tonight.

Break a leg

Violet: Thx. Do u have a stuft dog?

McKenzie: ?

Violet: We lost toto

Thirty seconds later, our costume manager told Mr. Goldstein that a nervous Munchkin had thrown up on four pairs of shoes. On the bright side, the Munchkin had missed Dorothy's ruby slippers.

With everyone distracted, I grabbed my Lion costume and ran outside, violating Mr. Goldstein's rules about keeping ourselves and our costumes backstage.

I unzipped the costume, turned it inside out, and frantically waved it in the fresh air to try to get rid of the stink.

After about eight strong waves, I put the costume near my nose and took a big whiff.

Yuck. Still disgusting.

I held the costume away from me as I walked back to the building.

My mom stood outside the door, carrying a spray bottle.

"What are you doing? Parents aren't allowed backstage,"

I said, even though Sarah's mother and Ally's grandpa were still here, and the vomiting Munchkin's mother was on her way with Tums and cleaning supplies.

"After you told me about your costume problems, I googled ways to freshen up sweat smells." Mom took my inside-out costume from me and wrinkled her nose. "You weren't kidding! This reeks!"

She held it away from us, pressed the tab of the spray bottle, and doused the costume.

"What's in there?" I asked.

"Water." Mom looked away from me. "And one other ingredient. Make sure you stay away from open flames."

I took my costume from her and sniffed it. There was just a slight odor now. "Much better. Thanks, Mom."

"You're welcome. I'll be rooting for you from the front row."

"Can I have the spray bottle?" I asked. "I'm not the only one with a smelly costume."

She shook her head.

"But—"

"That other ingredient . . ." Mom leaned in and whispered, "Supposedly, the best thing for removing odors from costumes is diluted vodka." She hugged me and hurried away.

When I came back inside, Sarah was pleading with Mr. Goldstein to let her wear a brown minidress instead of her ugly burlap Scarecrow costume, while he said, "No, no, no, no, no, no."

I had just gotten into my costume and makeup when McKenzie rushed into the dressing room. She held up a plastic bag. "I brought Toto. He's the only stuffed dog I have." She pulled out a large stuffed Scooby-Doo dog that had seen better days. It also had seen better years—probably better decades, too. Its fur was faded and frayed, its left eye and right ear were missing, and it had neck tattoos of crooked red hearts. The thing was too big for Dorothy's basket. It might scare young children in the audience. Plus, it wasn't a dark terrier like the famous movie Toto. It was Scooby-Doo.

McKenzie handed him to me. "Give him back when you're done with him, okay?"

"Why?" I couldn't help asking.

"This guy slept on my bed from, like, the time I first got a bed until . . . well, he still sleeps on my bed. And I used to take him with me everywhere, even to my dad's funeral."

I held him carefully against my chest. McKenzie was a good friend. "Thank you so much. He'll make a great Toto."

McKenzie nodded like it was nothing, said, "Break a leg," and left me and Scooby.

I hurried over to the props manager and said, "If you can't find Toto, you'll have to use this."

He frowned. "That decrepit Scooby-Doo?"

"Yes." If that didn't motivate him to find our Toto, nothing would.

I handed him Decrepit Scooby and said, "I know he's old and ratty, but he's my friend's beloved stuffed animal. So treat him with care."

On my way back to the greenroom, I saw Ally in her Dorothy costume, leaning against the hallway wall, staring at the script and mumbling her lines again.

"Ally," I said.

She looked at me. Her eyes were even redder than they'd been at lunchtime.

I grabbed her script and started walking.

"What are you doing?" Ally sounded panicked.

"Follow me." I headed toward the exit.

"No one is to leave!" Mr. Goldstein called after us. "There are only twelve minutes until show time and—"

I was out the door.

Ally followed me. She tried to snatch back the script.

I held it away from her. "If you don't know your lines twelve minutes before you go onstage, you're not going to suddenly learn them now."

"I'm doomed!" Ally cried.

"But you *do* know your lines. I've heard you in rehearsals."

Ally shook her head.

"You got stage fright yesterday, that's all. Remember, bad dress means good show."

"Ha!" Ally said.

"Listen." I stared into her red eyes. "I looked up that quote today in the computer lab. The bad dress/good show thing is real. There's a long Wikipedia article on it. They called the dress rehearsal for *Les Misérables* "Lake Misery" because it was so bad, and then the show became one of the hugest successes ever. And you know how Carrie Underwood did *Sound of Music* live on TV? Well, at the dress rehearsal she tripped over her guitar case and got a big gash on her leg. Plus, she forgot the words to that yodeling song. And when she kissed the guy who played the captain, she drooled on him. A lot. Her drool even got on his shirt."

"Really?" Ally's red eyes widened.

I nodded. "Look, we fixed everything. We have a Toto. My mom cleaned my costume." I didn't mention that Toto was Decrepit Scooby-Doo or that I was in danger of bursting into flames.

Ally smiled faintly.

"And you're a fantastic actor and singer," I added. "Plus, everyone in the cast and crew cares about you a lot. No matter what. We're a caring family."

She hugged me. "And you're a caring friend. I feel so much better now. You're a superhero."

Not exactly, I thought. *But sometimes I was pretty super. Sometimes you could even call me a hero.*

Right after we returned to the greenroom, Sarah Blanchette shouted, "Henry Tomaselli's dad fixed the stage curtain!"

"Maybe everything really will go okay," Ally said.

I nodded. In any case, I had confidence in my acting and adlibbing skills. I'd just made up all that stuff about *Les*

Misérables and Carrie Underwood. I hadn't even gone to the computer lab today.

And if we were awful, I knew a great real estate agent who could sell our house and buy something thousands of miles away.

"Two minutes until show time!" Mr. Goldstein's panicked voice called out as if he were shouting, *Two minutes until the nuclear bomb goes off!*

I should have given him a drink from my mom's spray bottle.

I ran to the stage curtain. Henry's dad was walking away with a large toolbox and a satisfied smile.

I peeked at the audience. My mom was there—front row, middle seat. She was always there for me. Sometimes she was there for me too much, but there were worse problems in life.

A few rows behind her sat Ally's grandparents/parents and her little sisters. McKenzie sat about eight rows back with Darcy Bollinger, Pearl something, and the girl whose name I always forgot.

I kept looking. I saw more friends from school and a few teachers.

I didn't see my dad. I hadn't expected him, not really. But I'd still hoped he'd come.

I gazed at my mom again. She was texting.

My phone buzzed.

Mom: Break a leg. I love you.

Violet: Thx

Mom: Seriously keep that ingredient secret and don't go near flames.

The lights dimmed, and I rushed to the greenroom to watch the start of the play on the monitor.

TWENTY-NINE

*E*veryone in the greenroom stared at the video monitor. The curtain opened perfectly, and we all seemed to exhale at once.

Ally stood downstage in her blue gingham pinafore. She clutched a tan wicker basket with Scooby-Doo duct-taped into it. The first scene went smoothly—no missed cues or Auntie M&Ms or sneezing fits—and the greenroom gang exhaled together again.

Then Ally was alone onstage, singing "Somewhere over the Rainbow." Her voice didn't sound like Judy Garland's. But it was lovely in its own way—sweet and honest—like Ally herself.

Right before the last verse, the one about happy blue-birds, the sound effects came in too early, drowning Ally's voice with a recording Mr. Goldstein's husband made at the senior center. The first sound was a loud gust of wind (actually, a blow dryer and a ceiling fan). Then Mr. Goldstein's husband's voice shouted, "Tornado!" An old man yelled, "Shelter down, Thelma," an old woman said, "Don't tell me what to do, Jerome," and another old woman said, "Keep it down. I'm trying to nap here." Finally, the recording shut off.

Ally ad-libbed: "Sounds like a tornado is coming. I'll just sing this last verse before going inside."

The audience laughed.

No one in the greenroom laughed.

Ally sang the last verse in a slightly shaky voice while I stared at the monitor and tried to send her encouraging thoughts.

"She'd better not ruin the play again," Sarah Blanchette muttered.

"Why don't you try being supportive," I said.

"Sarah, you're on in a few minutes," Diego said from behind her. "You need to get ready."

Sarah bent down and stared at the chair next to her. "Where's my Scarecrow minidress? I put it right here."

"The dress Mr. Goldstein told you not to wear?" I asked.

"You hid it, didn't you, Violet? Where is it?" Sarah demanded.

I crossed my arms over my Lion costume, which was just as hideous as Sarah's Scarecrow costume. "I swear on my great-grandma's grave, I didn't touch your little dress."

"You're going to miss your cue," Diego said.

Onstage, Glinda the Good Witch welcomed Dorothy to Munchkin Land. Backstage, Sarah cursed out Diego and me before running to the wings.

Diego and I burst out laughing.

"I spy a missing dress," I said. I pointed to Diego's lumpy right calf.

He bent down, rolled up his silver Tin Man pants leg, and took out the scrunched-up dress. "How did that get there?" he asked with a smile.

As he returned Sarah's dress to the chair, I stared at the video monitor, relieved that Ally seemed to have gotten her confidence back.

A few minutes later, Sarah stood onstage singing "If I Only Had a Brain." Her costume really was ugly—a shirt and pants made from brown burlap bags with pieces of straw glued on them, a thick belt, and an orange pointy hat. But scarecrows weren't supposed to be cute. They were supposed to scare crows. Sarah sang like the Scarecrow in the movie, except a lot angrier.

Diego played the Tin Man with a silly, squeaky voice. Each time Dorothy moved his limbs, he said "Ow!" or "*¡Ay, caramba!*" or "Oy vey!" The audience laughed like crazy. Phew.

When he got serious in his song about wishing for a heart, I felt my own heart swell.

Then it was time for my big "Courage" song. I stood downstage and opened my mouth, but nothing came out. I peered into the dark at the audience. I could only see the first few rows. I could tell that Mom was worried. I could also tell that she could tell that I was worried.

Ally thinks I have a pretty voice, I told myself. *Mr. Goldstein said I'm splendid. Plus, I've practiced this song a quadrillion times. And the most important thing, even more important than what Ally and Mr. Goldstein think of me, is that deep down I know I'm good.*

I started singing. I *was* good. As I sang about being a lion instead of a mouse, I realized I'd become much more like a brave lion than a timid mouse. I'd refused to quit the play when McKenzie asked me to. I'd summoned up the courage to apologize to Ally and tell off my dad. And now I had the nerve to belt out this song in front of a quadrillion strangers and, even scarier, people I knew.

The applause at the end of my solo was loud and long— long enough to bask in.

Then Ally, Diego, Sarah, and I skipped around the stage, arm in arm. We took three extra laps as we waited and waited for the green spotlight.

When it finally came on, we exclaimed that we must be nearing the Emerald City and sang "We're Off to See the Wizard."

The curtain closed, shakily this time, for intermission. The first act of the play was over, and we'd survived. Actually, we'd thrived.

THIRTY

PROBLEMS IN ACT TWO OF THE PLAY

1. The Munchkin who was sick before the play admitted he'd barfed on the Toto prop and thrown it behind some bushes, so we were stuck with Scooby-Doo Toto.

2. When the Wicked Witch came onstage, a little kid cried in terror. The Wicked Witch said, "This is Mr. Goldstein's fault. He made me do the play tonight."

3. Monkey #2 broke up with Monkey #1 during intermission, causing Monkey #1 to play her part with tears streaming down her face.

GOOD THINGS ABOUT THE PLAY

1. My costume didn't burst into flames.

2. We remembered almost all our lines.

3. The person who blew the most lines was Sarah.

4. The play went a lot better than the dress rehearsal.

5. We got a standing ovation.

GREAT THINGS ABOUT THE PLAY

I. During the final bow, when the whole cast held hands, I stood next to Diego.

2. Our hands fit perfectly together, as if they were made for each other.

3. Diego and I held hands longer than anyone else, standing silently behind the curtain after it had shakily closed. Finally, Diego gave my hand a little squeeze and let go. Then we ran off. It was the most romantic minute of my life.

When I got to the girls' dressing room, Ally grinned at me and exclaimed, "We did it!"

"I knew we could," I said.

"I didn't," she said.

The door opened wide, and McKenzie walked in.

"Actors only," Sarah said with a sneer. "No fan girls allowed."

"I'm definitely not your fan girl," McKenzie shot back.

Ally and I giggled.

McKenzie rushed over to me and gave me a quick hug. "Congratulations! Good show!"

"Thanks. We couldn't have done it without your Scooby." I handed him to her.

"True, McKenzie. We really needed him," Ally said.

"You did terrific tonight, Ally," McKenzie said.

"Thanks. I'm glad you came," Ally said. "I need to go. My family's waiting for me and it's way past my sisters' bedtime."

"If you want to stay longer, I bet my mom could drive you home," I said.

"Yeah." McKenzie nodded. "Violet's mom is always driving people home. She's great."

"Ask your parents," I told Ally. "We can sit in the back seat together and talk."

After Ally walked out, McKenzie said, "I shouldn't have quit the play. I might not be the most talented person, but I could have acted like a monkey without sobbing."

I laughed. "Hey, you want to sleep over tomorrow night?"

"Sure," McKenzie said. "Did your dad come to the play?"

"Highly doubtful," I said.

"Sorry."

"It's okay. I'm over it."

McKenzie raised her eyebrows. "Highly doubtful. We can talk about it tomorrow night. Or call me before then."

I nodded. "Thanks."

"You should go greet your fans and enjoy your Horton

Johnson Middle School fame," McKenzie said. "And I'd better leave before Sarah reports me for trespassing."

Right after McKenzie left, my mom walked in. She hugged me. "You were fantastic! I loved the play!"

I stepped out of the hug because I had a low tolerance for parental public displays of affection. I said, "We made a lot of mistakes."

"Really? I didn't notice," Mom lied. Then she said, "Violet, do you know your father is here? I saw him at intermission."

My heart pulsed, not in the achy way it felt lately when I thought about Dad, but in a fluttering butterfly way. I couldn't help asking Mom, "Did you sit together?"

She shook her head.

My butterflies drooped a little.

"I need to get out of this costume," I said. Dad wasn't a patient person. It would be awful if he left while I was still in the dressing room.

"I'll wait in the auditorium," Mom said.

I scrubbed off my makeup before she even left the room. Then I threw on my jeans and T-shirt and hurried out.

The auditorium was mostly empty. My parents stood in

the aisle about ten rows back, talking and leaning in to each other—only about a five-degree angle for each of them, but I could see it.

I took a few quiet steps toward them. My heart did the fluttery butterfly thing again. I'd fantasized about this—Dad coming to my play and talking to Mom.

Except in my fantasy, my parents were sitting, and Dad had his arm around Mom. I'd also pictured a big bouquet of roses on Mom's lap.

I hadn't fantasized about what their faces would look like, but they wouldn't have been tight-lipped and narrow-eyed like they were now. I'd never imagined Dad taking out his phone and staring at it while Mom picked at her cuticle.

I walked toward Mom and Dad, my fluttery butterflies replaced by stinging wasps. Even though I hadn't seen my parents together in months, walking toward them, toward their unhappiness, felt so awfully familiar. Just another night of trying to get between them and head off one of their fights. The stinging wasps felt familiar too. Why had I thought things could change?

"Hey, Dad," I said, my voice shakier than I'd wanted it to be.

He looked up from his phone. He had grown short fuzzy hairs on the lower half of his face. I didn't know if he wanted to grow a beard or didn't feel like shaving. He also had pierced his nose. The round red stud in it looked like a zit.

He gave me a giant smile and grabbed me in a bear hug.

I hugged him back. I completely forgot about his phone scrolling and hair scruff and pierced nose and my low tolerance for parental public displays of affection. It just felt so good, like old times. I basked in Dad's hug like I'd basked in the applause.

When the hug ended, I was so keyed up I could barely think. Except I noticed Mom had walked away.

"Vi, the apple of my eye," Dad said. "You were terrific! Quite the actress!"

"Did you like my song? I was nervous at first. I bet you could tell."

His smile faded a little, and he blinked fast a few times.

My smile faded completely. I glared at Dad's silly, selfish face and asked, "What time did you get here?"

"Intermission," he said quietly.

I folded my arms. "You missed my big song."

"I wanted to get here sooner, but . . ." His voice trailed off. "I had important—"

"*I'm* important!" I half shouted.

Then I took a deep breath and stared at my dad, not at his nose stud and chin fuzz this time, but at his eyes. They were the same shape and color as mine, except they seemed sad and they had wrinkles around them, more wrinkles than I'd remembered.

I'd spent the last few months—most of my life, really— expecting the Wizard of Oz. I'd discovered the Man Behind the Curtain.

"You *are* important." Dad stared right back at me. His eyes got shiny and he started blinking fast again, but this time he was blinking back tears. Then he said in a voice as sad as his eyes, "You deserve more than I've given you, Vi."

I nodded. I did deserve more. I said, "I'm glad you came tonight. To the last half of the play, anyway." My voice came out a little sad, though not as sad as his.

My dad had a lot of faults. But I wouldn't rank him on the bottom of my list of Dad Situations from Bad to Worst. Besides, I'd realized that ranking people on lists doesn't really work. Relationships are much too complicated, even for a math genius.

"You can come to my apartment and sing the show songs for me," he said. "A special command performance."

"When? Tomorrow?" I asked quickly without thinking.

Dad looked away and took his time to respond. "Someday soon," he answered.

I bit my lip. Why did figuring himself out mean abandoning me? Mom had figured out how to make herself into a great real estate agent while still driving me to school and making dinner and stuff.

"Fine," I said. "I'm going back to my friends."

Dad reached out to hug me again, but I turned and walked away.

I plodded up the aisle toward McKenzie and Ally, who were talking about twelve rows back, and Mom, who stood by herself a few rows behind them. The closer I got, the faster I walked.

I hadn't brought my parents together. I never would. I didn't even want to anymore. But I'd brought McKenzie and Ally together. And I'd sung onstage in front of hundreds of people while wearing ugly yellow makeup and an even uglier lion costume. Plus, I hadn't collapsed when Diego held my hand. And I'd done something that took even more nerve: I told my dad I was important.

You might not call any of those things heroic feats. I wasn't the bravest person in the world. I was just Violet: loyal friend, math genius, good singer, homework-challenged student, bold/needy daughter, and far from cowardly.

THIRTY-ONE

*W*hen I reached Mom, Ally, and McKenzie in the auditorium, Mom said, "How about I take you girls to celebrate at Sunshine Desserts on the way home?"

"Sounds great to me," I said. Sunshine Desserts meant pie.

"Me too!" McKenzie and Ally said.

Ally called her parents and got permission. McKenzie told Ally she didn't need permission because her mom was part of the Free-Range Kids Movement. Mom and I bit our lips while she said it.

The four of us piled into Grandpa Falls-Apart. Mom acted as chauffeur and McKenzie, Ally, and I sat in the back. I didn't even mind being squeezed in the middle of the back seat with my skinny butt perched on the hard bump, because my two best friends were on either side of me. Plus, the pie factor.

As Mom drove out of the school parking lot, I said, "Sunshine Desserts makes an apple-berry pie to die for."

"She really means that," McKenzie said. "Violet would lay down her life for that pie."

"Don't be ridiculous. If I was dead, I couldn't eat pie," I said. "I'd only sacrifice a small body part for it, like a tonsil or pinky toe."

Everyone laughed.

"I'm so glad the play's over," Ally said. "I never want to star in a play again. Way too much pressure."

McKenzie gave a little snort. It was too dark to see, but I knew she was rolling her eyes too.

"I'm lucky I got cast though," Ally said, probably in response to the snort. "I just felt awful every time I screwed up. Which was a lot."

"No, it wasn't," McKenzie said.

"No one's perfect," I added sort of automatically. Then I thought about it. There's a lot to that expression. No one's life is perfect, and no one acts perfectly either. Ally had whined about getting to star in the play. McKenzie had kicked me in the cafeteria. Dad missed the first half of the play. Mom had emailed me pretending to be Dad.

And I was far from perfect. I'd made quadrillions of mistakes.

$$\text{Life} = \text{Mistakes} \times 10^{15}$$

My biggest mistake was being so scared of making mistakes that I didn't do stuff—like stand up to my dad, or ask McKenzie about her mom, or tell my mom I appreciated her.

As we walked into Sunshine Desserts, Mom said, "I love the decor here." Only a realtor would care about decor at the best pie place in Orange County.

"It's nice," McKenzie said. "But the light fixtures could use some updating. And I'd suggest crown molding."

Mom and I sat on one side of the table, with Ally and McKenzie on the other.

"I hope they have sweet potato pie," Ally said. "That's my favorite."

Sweet potatoes don't deserve to be in the same sentence as pies, let alone inside them! How could that be Ally's favorite? I stared wide-eyed at her and hoped this wouldn't hurt our friendship.

McKenzie started giggling.

A second later, Ally was giggling too. Between giggles, Ally pointed to McKenzie and said, "She told me to say that."

I laughed and shook my head at them.

After some internal debate, I ordered a slice of my usual: apple-berry pie à la mode, which was never less than amazing. McKenzie also ordered her usual: chocolate pecan pie with whipped cream. Mom ordered banana cream pie, and Ally ordered razzleberry pie with whipped cream.

When the slices arrived, McKenzie, Ally, and I traded forkfuls. We each decided we liked our own order best.

Mom ate only about 30 percent of her pie and let us split the rest. Banana cream pie barely made my top twenty list. But it still tasted delicious.

I was so grateful, I told Mom, "Now that we've celebrated the play with pie, we should celebrate your real estate deal with sushi."

"That would be fun," Mom said, looking surprised.

"Not fun for the fish," McKenzie said. "If sushi is raw fish, does that mean the fish is alive when you eat it?"

"No," Mom said. "Not usually, anyway."

Ew. If only Dad had taken Mom for sushi, I wouldn't have to.

Taking someone to a raw-fish restaurant just because it's

their favorite may be the definition of true love. Since my dad had refused to do it, I should have known that saving my parents' marriage was mathematically impossible. And I shouldn't have tried to solve my parents' problems with math.

I should have solved my *own* problems with math. I'd made so many charts, but my focus had been off. It was like endlessly trying to calculate the exact amount of pi instead of using pi to discover more about circles and spheres, which is the real point. I'd focused on the subtraction and division of broken homes and fractured friendships, but I should have been thinking about the addition and multiplication of new friends and growing relationships.

As we sat at the café, talking and laughing and sharing whipped cream and ice cream, I realized life is like a pie chart—it always fills up. When one slice gets thinner or even disappears, another slice expands to takes its place. And the new slice may be even better than the old one. So you have to be willing to try new things. Maybe one day I'd even order Sunshine Desserts's lima bean pie and find out I like it.

Well, the odds of that happening were about quadrillion to one.

I looked around the table, at my mom and my best friends. You can learn a lot about life from pie charts, but you can learn even more from people. The very best kind of pie chart is one filled with people, especially the people who filled up my life now.

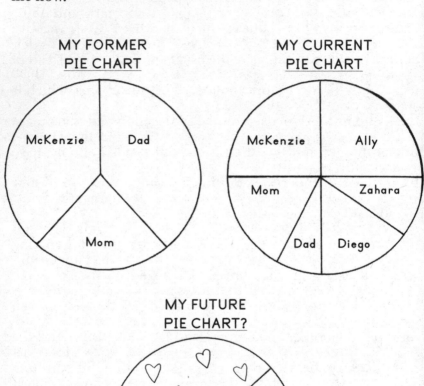

MY FORMER
PIE CHART

MY CURRENT
PIE CHART

MY FUTURE
PIE CHART?

ACKNOWLEDGMENTS

Start with my mother, Judy Green, who's as sweet as pie.

Add Jeff Garfinkle's support, as infinitc as pi.

Add the blessings of my children, Sarah, Mark, and Aaron.

Add love and laughter from my writer sisterhood, Marlene Perez, Alyson Noel, Stacia Deutsch, Priya Ardis, Debbi Michiko Florence, and April Henry.

Then add critiques and compassion from Denny Holland, Louella Nelson, Beverly Plass, Kristin James, Brad Oatman, Herb Williams-Dalgart, Debra Gaal, Susan Angard, Laurie Casey, Begoña Echeverria, David Collins, Jody Feldman, Mary Beth Miller, Cinda Chima, Martha Levine, Pam Gruber, and mighty junior critiquers Darcy, Megan, and Maddy.

Multiply that sum by dream agent Sarah Davies.

Multiply again by crème de la crème editor Sally Morgridge. Add the Holiday House heroics of Kerry Martin, Pamela Glauber, and Mary Cash.

The result: the luckiest writer alive.